The Consultant

Kevin Dinwoodie

To my wife and all those who made this possible.

Other books by Kevin Dinwoodie

Comfy Monkey

1

I don't know if all industries have consultants, but many have, so why shouldn't criminals have a consultant? Sherlock Holmes provides balance here, describing himself as a 'consulting detective' and this is a tale of a consulting criminal. But I need to be careful regarding the incriminating details. I know the difference between good and bad and between bad and evil. I will cross the line of legality when I feel it is advantageous and safe for me to do so and I keep a few tenets of my own to save guilt. I don't arrange deaths, I keep away from drugs and I always keep a secret. Always. And I expect those I decide to work with to take their secrets to their grave too.

The services I provide within those strictures are varied, but as per other consultants, I have a network of contacts. I hide these under an elaborate matrix of codes and varied cell phones and have built trust with my clients and customers. Even in this internet age and the dark web, the personal touch of knowing who to trust is a valuable commodity. So, I can be contacted through various means and asked to arrange a service or provide information. A fee is paid or a commission received and secrecy, professionalism and deniability is maintained. I do also take a more hands-on approach in some jobs and take an agreed slice of the pie, but these must involve a large pie to balance the risk and reward, to ensure the return on my investment. This tale covers a massive pie and lets you know some secrets that I am happy to let you into. Any names, locations and characters used in the following are fictitious. Probably…

Part I – Analysis

2

The Consultant had an open-door approach to potential customers. If you were 'in the know' then you could usually find him on a Tuesday in the same pub, at the same time. The table may differ, dependent on times of the year (Cheltenham Gold Cup week usually disrupts things; in a good way) but today he sat at his favourite table in his favourite pub, The Beehive (the one in Montpellier not Prestbury). The set up was always the same. He sat facing the door, in the corner of the snug, the bench allowed someone to sit beside him and share his table without drawing attention. He would try to have about quarter of a pint left, enough to say, if offered a drink, 'no, I have that to finish' or to say 'aye, I will have another'. He had two papers, the Financial Times and the Racing Post. If you couldn't walk up to a stranger in a pub with those on the table and not think of an opening to strike up an innocent conversation, then you would need more help than the Consultant could provide. He would often read a book rather than the papers, (they were mere props) whilst waiting for customers to approach. This route was old fashioned as he received many approaches via the dark web, but people do like the personal service.

A guy in his late twenties sat down a little way off. He had put the smart in 'smart casual', spending some cash on looking good. You could say he was well-manicured, but actually his hands let him down. He was fit and tanned. Manual labour, cash-in-hand and outside work came to mind. This was gleaned with sideways looks but then their gazes crossed and there was a nod of acknowledgement.

"You a betting man?" came from the fella with a general point of the index finger of the hand holding his pint towards the Racing Post.

"That could apply to shares or horses" said the Consultant with a smile and a nod of the head, "but we all prefer to deal in certainties."

That opening gambit seemed to work for them both and the fella continued, gingerly.

"We may have a common acquaintance?" It did hang as a question as the two of them felt their way and the Consultant liked the term 'acquaintance' and nodded to encourage more.

"Who would that be?" A name was mentioned. "If I were to contact them, what would they say about you?"

The visitor was not expecting that question, he would have to describe how he perceived how others saw him. He should answer truthfully, but also he needed something from the Consultant. He dodged the question.

"Well, I must be trustworthy otherwise he would not have sent me to see you. And I think our mutual friend must like me as he has helped me, to send me your way."

"Do you work for him?"

"Only to clean his windows."

The Consultant raised his eyebrows with surprise and whilst this explained to the Consultant the poor fingernails, it wasn't a profession that he offered, or needed services from. But it offered a codename, this guy would become Glazier.

"And why did he send you to see me?" Glazier seemed to ponder the best reply and shrugged as he said "it's all a bit strange, I kinda need some help, but I am not too sure what with." The Consultant thought that was vague. Their mutual contact was a small-time burglar that was careful with what jobs he took on, there was an easy link from a window cleaner to a burglar, one would have a great view of contents and the other could make the most of the information...but not too often or the link would be obvious to everyone.

The Consultant listened enough to judge a) if he can help and b) if he wanted to help. So far no judgement either way had been made, so it was time for him to ask for more.

"OK, I may be able to assist, tell me more of the proposition but be vague and mention no names or anything specific that others could tie us into in the future. It seems that you are a window cleaner so you will go by the name Glazier. I am the Consultant. Whilst I don't want to know much about you, have you been to prison?"

"Young offenders, two months. Do you want to know what for?"

"No that's not necessary. But you are not on probation or out on licence now?"

"No. I really have put all that behind me. My time inside was enough and I'm clean as a whistle now." They both exchanged a look and shuffled in their seats as they knew that was a lie. "If I do anything I shouldn't then it's taking cash. I rarely see that in the houses I clean windows for, but if I spot a large stash then it's a mental note or I can refer it to our mutual friend." There was a nod of understanding.

"But our mutual friend is not interested in this proposition. What's strange about it?"
Glazier got himself comfortable and leaned into their shared table and the Consultant moved the papers aside in a metaphorical clearing of a path between them. "I have a commercial contract to clean windows at an office, each quarter and nothing too odd, apart from all windows are mirrored and barred. There is a plate glass door, but that leads to a reception and no-one seems to use that. All the other doors are thick, secure and tight." A gesture was made with clenched fist to emphasis the building was

secure. "Anyhow…one of the managers came to me one day and chats over what a good job I do and he asks if I would be interested in an additional job, 'yes' I say and he says that they sometimes like packages to go to other addresses. All I would need to do is to receive the package and bring it to their office and then clean the windows. So come and clean the windows and drop off the package. I then increase my regular invoice by a hundred pounds to cover the inconvenience." Glazier leaned in further and continued "so that sounded fine to me, clearly they wanted to hide the fact that I was delivering these packages and something fishy was going on, I knew there was more to it…so I asked 'what was the catch?' He then explained the rules and these just made me realise how fishy this was. Rule one, I have to give them a week's notice if I am going away; two, I have two days from me receiving the package to my delivering it to them; three, don't tamper with the package. It's not for me. I am not to open it. Each one is photocopied at its despatch and has unique wrapping. They will know if it's opened. So I ask 'what is in it' and he says, it's nothing illegal, they just want to manage their supply lines, but it is important that they know what was sent will be with them promptly and unmolested…so the packages are sealed in a way that is tamperproof. So, whilst I am not taken-in by the 'nothing illegal' it's a hundred pounds extra, so I'm in. The package arrives at my home address by Royal Mail, they have that red card through the door if I am out, it all looks fine." He uses his hands to indicate a rectangular box, perhaps the size of a litre juice carton. "They have my address on a laser printed label, they are well stuck down with a patterned duct tape that's overlapped, so there would be no way to repackage it. And the postmarks vary but are from Belgium, Luxembourg and Holland." And with that he leaned back picked up his pint and raised his shoulders in a 'make of that what you will'

7

gesture, then emphatically took the last of his drink.

"How often do they come?"

"About every two months, their windows are spotless by the way."

"How heavy are they?"

"Not very, they do vary, but about quarter of a kilo."

"And what happens when you deliver them?"

"Well. We have a routine. I put the package in my bucket before I leave home, when I arrive I go into their loading bay to get some water. I take my bucket with me and hand the package to their security guy and he takes it into their office."

"You said the windows are mirrored and barred and now they have a security guy too?"

"Yep, he works through the day. At night, from what I have seen, it's an alarm and physical security, which is quite good. The reception door had ram-raid bollards outside, but as I said I have never seen that door being used. Everyone seems to use the loading bay, and that's where the security guy is. At night the shutters are down and there is a side door, but that's like a fire door." He looked intently at the Consultant here and wiggled his head to see if his point got across and decided he needed to provide more. "A fire door, one of those doors with nothing on the outside, no handle, lock, keyhole, nothing. But on the inside a push bar…and people use that to leave, but most of us just walk through the loading bay."

"So, from the loading bay you can get into the office?"

"Yep, but there are doors there. The one from the loading bay is a big door, heavy metal and a *good lock*…" (the Consultant took the emphasis on 'good lock' to mean some professional respect from someone who knew his locks) "…that's the good physical security I mentioned.

During the day it's open and I have stood there and seen the package go through that door. After the door there is a kitchen on the left, so I have had a coffee made for me there. Beyond that there is a gate, floor to ceiling barred gate and I have only seen that locked, the security guy passes the package through the bars and further up is another solid looking door."

"And beyond that, any ideas?"

"Only once did I get a glimpse of what was beyond." Glazier adjusted himself on his seat, shuffling forward to get closer to the Consultant again, but also displaying his discomfort in what he was going to say. "It was really quick, a lady opened the door and came down the corridor, so all I got was a view between her and the door frame. I saw a big safe. Like a vault safe. Walk in one, or a large cupboard. Big and it had two combination dials on it and two door handles."

"So, a big, double-door safe that has *something* in it. Three doors in one corridor, that are all accessed from a loading bay that's alarmed and that's protected by a guard?"

"Yep, that's the size of it…but" and Glazier raised his hands palms outwards in a look of surrender "I don't want to go in while the guard is there, he's a nice bloke, makes me coffee, supports Southampton…" he looked at the Consultant with a sharp stare "forcing him to open up isn't what I had in mind."

"I am happy with that, I suspect that you know how I work. Quiet. In and out." The two nodded in tacit agreement. Breaking heads and guns blazing was for the movies. "So how do you plan to get in?"

"I don't rightly know."

The Consultant and Glazier leaned back into their own seats and considered. This kind of conundrum, to plan a way around an issue and bring in experts from their own fields to assist, is what the Consultant does best. Lots of questions were running through his head, most he parked for later but then Glazier continued with a beaming smile on his face and he leaned in again.

"But the good news is that I do have a key for the first door." He paused for effect, if he had a key then that was one part of the puzzle. "If I see an opportunity to get an impression of a key to a house with valuables then that's something I can use, so I carry blu tack so that I am prepared. I said the guard gets me coffee and passed the package through the grill of the gate. That's when I got an impression of the key. He unlocked the door, propped it open and left his keys in it."

Silence settled into their corner of an otherwise rather boisterous bar and the consultant pondered and quickly decided that he couldn't decide anything yet.

"Do you have a package with you?"

"No, I didn't bring it with me. But, as luck would have it, I did have one delivered today so I will deliver it tomorrow."

"Excellent. This is what I will do. I am going to ask our mutual friend about your references and if all's well then we will meet outside here tomorrow at ten. Dress smart. If you have a suit then wear it…and if your references don't check out then I will be a no-show. If I decide this isn't something I can assist with then again I will be a no show." Glazier wasn't sure if he should be relieved, thankful or worried. The Consultant studied him as all these feelings and thoughts crossed Glazier's mind. You could see him spot a realisation off in the distance, you could see his excitement. A small smile appeared and he said "Cool, see you tomorrow then."

3

Glazier looked nervous. Wearing a suit was unfamiliar to him so he adjusted his tie and collar as they waited in the vestibule of some rather swanky offices. Marble, glass and chrome abounded and the welcome heating gave a gentle hiss in counterpoint to the revolving door's swish and pop. The two of them fitted in, other users of the office came and went, both male and female wore suits too and Glazier and the Consultant were camouflaged in the company of company people. Some were waved-through security and others garnered more scrutiny; they had been held while others were inspected and finally, when all others had been processed and they sat alone, the pair were ushered brusquely forward by a broad security guard. He was dressed in a uniform that shone brightly and was on good terms with a hot iron. He wasn't young, Glazier felt he could outrun him, which would be the best option as he looked handy in a fight. But neither of them would want blood on their shirts; his was new and the security guard's looked like it took an age to iron.

The guard led them aside and into an alcove that revealed a luggage X-ray machine, smaller than those in an airport, but recognisable none-the-less. The three routinely gathered at the end of the machine, the guard opened the conversation.

"Long-time-no-see, I thought you had forgotten about me."

"Just not had need of your services, I am glad to say that the market for suspect packages isn't what it used to be." As this was said the consultant placed an envelope onto the bed of the machine and the guard swept it into his pocket in a slow and gentle movement. Both then looked at Glazier, who was perplexed at what to do next. The Consultant's usual approach to most things was 'less said the better' so Glazier had just attended as asked, dressed smartly and had placed the package in a brief case that the

11

consultant had provided and Glazier had then carried. Then Glazier got it.

"Oh yes, you want this don't you" and went to remove the packet from the briefcase. The Consultant raised a steadying hand as the guard said "no need to take it out, whatever it is…that's what the machine is for."

'*Oh yeah, good point*' thought Glazier and the three of them moved to look at the screen as the briefcase and its contents glided into view. The guard changed the intensity and clarity, pushed a button, then reversed the conveyor so that the briefcase re-appeared from whence it had come. He then turned the briefcase over and took it back into the machine. Again, some adjustment with button pushing and the output of that function was then revealed as two still photographs of the internals of the package. The contents of the package were revealed. They all strained to look.

"It's something dense wrapped in bubble wrap, plenty of wrap to fill the package, you can see the size of it, does that help you gauge the weight, metal over powder for example?" That was the expert opinion from the guard. "I can check for drugs?" Consultant thought this through and nodded as the image, size and weight could point to packed powder and he wanted to avoid drugs, he opened the suitcase and the guard prepared a part of the machine that evidently sniffed the package. A small cloth was placed (using tweezers) within a ladle shaped wand wired to the machine. The bowl of the ladle was moved around the package, the cloth being rubbed against all parts of the package. When the guard was satisfied that a sample was collected the cloth was removed, again with tweezers. It was placed in another part of the machine and the guard turned to the men.

"Unless they scrubbed it with bleach, this will detect something. It's very sensitive, even if someone has handled something they shouldn't and then they touched this package, it'll flag it." He studied a screen where clearly results would appear and then he continued with some finality. "No drugs. And the good news keeps coming, no explosives."

4

"So, what's next?" was the question hanging in the air. Glazier posed it as they walked down the steps of the office and turned back towards where his van was parked. They walked side by side, two men in suits, one had a briefcase, both smart in more than one way. Both thinking 'so what *is* next?' The Consultant had spotted and not avoided the body language, they were walking as equals, potentially planning the next move.

He had called their mutual friend. Glazier had been vouched for in a limited way but the key for the Consultant was that there was history. Glazier had been known for some time, he had local roots, he was remembered and had not just appeared in Cheltenham from another policing region. The Consultant knew that the police had wanted to implicate and arrest him for several crimes that he had been involved in and many more that he wasn't. A honey trap was always around the corner; at least that was the way he approached cold callers.

"I'm not sure, more analysis is needed." That was a catch-all delaying tactic. He had hoped that the X-ray would have answered questions but they had not moved on much. But he wanted to be optimistic and positive. It wasn't explosives and it wasn't drugs and it was clearly something of value. He was interested. He wanted to know more before he thought about getting involved.

"I think you had better deliver the package, I have a change of clothes back at my car, it's by the pub. Can we go now?" The Consultant was careful what he carried in his own car, as 'going equipped' to commit a crime could include mundane tools in a car, but a change of clothes was something that he felt less worried about. When they got to his car he changed in the street, slipped his shirt off, put on a black tee and black jacket. He was also pleased that his request to 'go now' was accepted. He still had to ensure that Glazier was trustworthy and his ability to react to sudden changes in plan was an indicator that he wanted to make this work. He climbed back into the van and saw that Glazier had changed too and was ready for work. It was a ubiquitous aging transit without logos or number on, just a rack with ladders and other paraphernalia on the roof.

"When we get close let me know and I will get into the back, just do whatever you normally do and I will see what I can from the back, that should be enough for me to get a feel of the place."

"Yep that's fine, I will open the side door and get my stuff out and leave it ajar and I normally park in the loading bay. It will be a while if I get to have a coffee and chat."

"You seem a bit too friendly at this place, are you sure you want to rob them?" Glazier seemed to see this as a strange question and took a moment.

"I like the guard. The owners are pleasant enough. I bet they are insured for whatever it is…so it's no real harm done."

"But we don't know what it is they are shipping in, it may be something they don't want to declare and insure. It could do some harm. We may aim to avoid harm, but the guard could be vulnerable, lose his job at the least?"

Glazier took some time to consider this and weigh up his thoughts on the pros and cons. "I'm here in this rusty transit, trying to make a living as being inside has put the kibosh on finding a decent job, one that involves your brain. I went self-employed as I was the only person who would give me a job. And the interview involved a great deal of psychoanalysis. But I have worked my ass off to get a deposit on a flat, to make rent, to get the business afloat but I am hanging on by my fingernails. A few side jobs that I risk do keep me going, but one mistake and I will be sunk again. I...and that could be *we*...may have something here that's big enough for me to..." he looked for the word, for the expression to express his thoughts "...breathe. You had best get in the back."

The Consultant did as instructed and pulled a balaclava from his jacket and retreated to the shadows of the van and ducked down.

The suburbs of Cheltenham had often engulfed trading estates that offered all types of trades spaces. Some very high-tech aerospace engineering occurred beside builder's merchants, auto mechanics and purveyors of sandwiches. In this case the valuable real estate of Cheltenham abruptly became warehousing and varied business and then an outlier, a detached unit with a reception, loading bay and mirrored windows high in an otherwise blank wall. It was small, the largest feature was the shutter on the loading bay, there was no company name emblazoned proudly, the reception did have an air of being unloved, but as a whole it was clean, tidy, set back and overtly unobtrusive. They approached slowly and turned into the bay. Two matching and late plate Mercedes saloons were parked line-astern at one side and the rusty transit snuggled in beside them. It became noticeably darker in the van as it passed into the building, it stopped short of the steps and elevated floor ahead. The back of the van was clear of the shutter but not by much. So the bay could take two vehicle side by side and offload onto the raised warehouse space beyond. Glazier hopped out and let light and air into the van through the sliding rear door and

15

took out the bucket wedged behind the front seat.

"You got my coffee on?" he shouted over his shoulder while looking for the Consultant in the gloom but then turned and pulled the door a little so a sideways view was offered. "You might as well whilst we get some hot water for the winders." The security guard and Glazier met at the front of the transit after Glazier leapt up to the loading level and started into the relaxed, genial, banter that guys who meet occasionally can have. The Consultant couldn't catch all the words but took the gist that coffee was on the way, football would be discussed and both were busy avoiding work. In the midst of this the package was exchanged and the heavy security door, on the left of where the Consultant was that led from the loading bay was unlocked. Glazier stayed external to this but they talked easily down the corridor.

To the right was a cabin for the guard. It was well lit and it was easy to see the CCTV screens, tapes and recorders. Tapes were reassuringly old-school, perhaps the other security was old too? He scanned what he could see without coming from the gloom. Through the side door he could see an alarm panel next to the fire door. A solid enough door and easy to open from the interior, impossible from the exterior. That panel and visible wiring inferred that the alarm would sound from motion of doors or windows being opened. The windows didn't seem to be an option as they were high, barred but they were very clean.

And that was it. He scanned again. Clean, empty, large expensive cars and plenty of security. As he looked at the fire door he noticed a large tool chest. Red, on wheels, the type with lots of drawers for lots of spanners. It was dusty and forgotten, from a past use of the premises. A thought crossed his mind and he spent some time getting as many photos of the view from the van as he could whilst Glazier carried out his very expensive window cleaning.

5

Glazier pulled himself into the driver's seat engaged gear, started and disengaged the clutch as one movement and searched behind for obstructions as he reversed and raised his hand in a farewell. A good display of muti-tasking. He also ignored the fact that the Consultant was back there in the shadows until they were some way off.

"So, what do you think?"

"It's as you described it" replied a voice from the gloom and the Consultant weaved through the contents of the van and into the passenger seat. "I'm intrigued. It isn't a place I know and I do pride myself on knowing a lot of other people's business, especially if it's not straight."

"Are we going to do it?"

"I don't think so" stated the Consultant emphatically. "You came to me as you cannot do the job yourself and I don't have all the capabilities needed. Can you crack a safe?" Glazier shook his head. "I didn't think so. So, are *we* going to do it? No. Can I get the team that we would need and build a plan; yes, I can do that." Glazier wasn't sure what to make of that, but then the Consultant added "I think it would be interesting to work out if it could be done." That did make Glazier smile. "However, it is one thing to think that a job can be done and another to say that it should be done. My worry is we don't know who these people are or what they are up to. I will look into it and then I will give you a ring and you can come and clean my windows and we can discuss. If you don't hear from me then it has not worked out but see me in the pub to check in if you want. Give me three weeks. As it stands, more analysis is needed."

6

Everyone declares some tax. Whole businesses consult on how to avoid tax, but some has to be paid. Paying no tax at all is a red rag to the capitalist state. The Consultant started his search in Companies House and Who Owns Whom to find accounts, returns and other info. It was as Glazier suggested. A family run business that paid some tax. An increasing amount over the years. A good amount but nothing stellar. Very stable and consistent. The more he looked the less surprises he found. It was very much in order and all the names he found and cross checked were related, it was a family concern, the company name was the initials of the founder and gave nothing away. It was unremarkable and involved in the import and export of "manufactured goods." If it was just money laundering then he would have expected more industry, more going on, something more obvious to allow the cash to flow. He researched other ideas but remained unconvinced that he knew what was in the packages.

The next step was surveillance. He hired a white transit and parked it in the industrial estate so that he again had a good view from the stygian gloom of the back of a transit. He brought food, papers, books, sleeping bag and pee bottles and stayed for two days.

The conclusion was that not many people worked there. The only regular was the security guard. He unlocked and put the shutters up at eight thirty each day. Just prior to nine a large Mercedes would arrive for the majority of the day. Two packages arrived whilst the Consultant was there. One was via Royal Mail and couldn't have been more straight-forward. The other was a guy who drove up in a spotless Range Rover and was so tubby he nearly rolled out of the driver's seat but walked in and handed over the package. Very off-handed way, not chatty and affable like Glazier, this was just a job to be done. Other Mercedes could arrive. They seemed to be the company car of choice. Leased, tax efficient perhaps. That tax consultant again. The drivers looked similar. Familiar names in the research were reflected in the familial look of builds and faces. If this was all within a family then that could help explain why no news was getting out on what they did.

A younger couple were also regular attendees, also in a Merc and looked to be part of the clan, but perhaps children or married in, leaner than the elder generation.

Every night the Mercedes saloons would leave, after their drivers had a genial chat with the guard and then he would lock up at five. The only thing the Consultant did spot and confirm on the second night was that carrying in a briefcase was no guarantee that you would carry one out.

During the inactivity of surveillance he considered that packages went in and something was coming out within briefcases. Some of the packages were legitimate and via Royal Mail and potentially others were off-book and clandestine. The legitimate route kept the linear increase in turnover and profits growing…but the amount that was hidden away was clearly well hidden.

None of his research to date showed any links to criminality that he had known of over the years. This seemed to be a store that he could turnover without troubling any of his previous and future customers.

So, it looked to be on. *If* he could get a team together. *If* they also agreed it could be done. But he had to convince himself and them to do a job when he was unsure what they were stealing. But, every journey starts with getting up out of a seat and all that…he would start at the hardest part. The safe.

19

7

Everyone loves allotments. They cut through the social barriers and brings communism (with a small c) to the villages within the Cheltenham conurbation. The demographic does lean to men who share a passion for gardening, football, cricket and getting away from the house for a long spell to join others with a thermos of tea and TMS or Five Live on the radio. Some may be escaping a wife and some are escaping the absence of a wife. For the Consultant and the man he was meeting it was the former. The allotment may not be a typical criminal's meeting point, but some criminals (and it is only the good ones) get old. With the Consultant's wealth of contacts he mixed with the up and coming, talented crooks, the experienced professionals and then there were the experts in their field. The professors if you will. Most of the criminals that get a mention in the news are the violent, young and inexperienced. Drug fuelled in many cases. These were avoided whenever necessary, the Consultant made his money and kept out of jail by working with professionals, who also wanted to make money and keep out of jail. But as Norman Stanley Fletcher knew, prison was an occupational hazard.

"How you doing Tom?"

"I am savouring my freedom."

"…but you have been out years now?"

"And I am making damn sure that you know that I am still savouring my freedom and don't want to go back in!" The Consultant hadn't heard something shouted so quietly before.

Tom was well dressed for the allotment. Fjällräven trousers, made for work, Aigle boots made for warmth, plus layers on his torso, he had been athletic in the past, but limped now, favouring his right side. His hair was cut short, military style as it had been since his recruitment many years ago. This man was considerably older than Glazier and had at least fifteen years on the Consultant. Any more serious prison time for him could mean life. The Consultant himself knew that this was a young man's game for many reasons. Keeping out of prison and harm's way takes energy and this man was putting his energy into weeding at this moment, hoeing as if the weeds themselves were snitches. But the pair had a legacy of success behind them, their trust in each other was unshakeable...and that was one reason the Consultant was here. But there was another reason, there were so few good safe crackers now, it would be good to get some succession planning arranged.

They were standing in one of the larger allotments, that Cheltenham holds. A relic from the times of its growth and its ability to spread from the Spa at its hub over virgin ground and provide plots in the suburbs for those coming to its long-gone factories. This one was not unusual in its plethora of well-tended and variegated contents, numerous old men prodding produce and folding themselves into the soil. Old professionals retire to their allotments. This old professional fitted the bill. Dapper and erect in past years, he was more slumped than previous and a three-year term at her Majesty's pleasure may not have helped there. But that was some time ago and nothing to do with the Consultant so he was a little shocked that his visit had been met with a voice that was raised to an extent that he knew the anger, but it was not overheard. Some judicious soil jabbing passed by as the Consultant thought of an approach.

"How's Joan?"

The prodding stopped for an iota then resumed at a slower pace and then stopped and Tom stood up to his full height, popping his vertebrae back into a row. He was wiry, over six foot and would have been someone to have avoided in his youth, or so the Consultant had been led to believe. But then Tom specialised and studied in safes and locks and he became very good at what he did. At this moment the glare that he levelled came from his youth.

"You had better not let her see you, I think she would be in the knife drawer and at you…and my wife with a knife is something to be seen."

"Thanks for the warning. I nearly came to the house but thought this might be more private. Anyway, I think Joan is lovely, I thought she had a soft spot for me? Why is she angry with me? She doesn't think I had anything to do with your time inside?"

"She does think you were involved. You know me. I don't grass. But I let her believe you were involved and didn't contradict. You know what happened, I copped for that job but didn't give anyone up, not even to Joan. She assumed it was your job, so you get the blackmark."

"But why have you got the hump with me?"

"Cos I made a mistake! I trusted to work with that twat who grassed me up and did three years and now I have retired and you're here to drag me back in!"

"So, you are really angry at yourself? And it looks like you are really pissed with that weed you've been jabbing your hoe at for five minutes."

The hoe was levelled in his direction and waggled "They were are all over me! You know what it's like, they get you on one job and every tickle from Plymouth to Perth involving a safe was put in-front of me. I was lucky to get from under it. Lucky. And I don't want to ride my luck."

"It wasn't luck. It was the fact that you kept your mouth shut, had good lawyers and had been careful over the years. The latter being the most important. You know I've always been good at that. Risk management. But I'm not going to bother you if you don't need it. If you have enough put aside." Neither of them had blinked since the mention of Tom's wife. The locked stare wasn't malevolent, it's just what happened, they had just locked eyes and kept going. A carrot had just been dangled. Tom wasn't a young guy out for the fun, experience or bravado. As with all professionals it was the money. If he needed some then more would be discussed. "I am not asking you to ride your luck, I don't want to take risks either, but there is something that we could work on together, if you are interested. It's an interesting task. Perplexing."

Tom exhaled and crumpled a little, he rubbed his soiled hand over his eyebrows. This saddened the Consultant as perhaps cash could tempt Tom from his planned retirement. The carrot had been nibbled.

"Good lawyers are not cheap and keeping your mouth shut loses its value if others don't. I've got a place in Portugal now." The change in tack surprised the Consultant, "I planned to retire there but my capital funding took a hit in that court case. My barrister doesn't know but my place is in the next village to his. At some point I may pop over and see if he has a safe and get my fee back. The renovations are expensive but nearly done. I can sell up here, that will release plenty for my twilight years…so I don't need another job."

"That's good, I don't like working with people who need things, I prefer to work with those who want things. Desperation is not a good motivation. This job has interest. You might want to do it."

"I am having a cuppa. Want one?" Tom moved towards his small shed and offered the door stop as a seat. This wasn't such a deprivation, the doorstop was a hefty tree stump that was a good size for a stool. Tom put a deckchair opposite the stump and with all the ceremony that could be made, fell into the folding chair, thermos in hand. They knew each other well, two good jobs behind them. 'Good' as in lucrative. No job could ever be 'good' if it got you caught and the two they had been within had been very clean. That knowledge of each other stretched to the tea and sugar was automatically added for the Consultant.

Tea in an allotment shed was a thing of beauty and they talked of brassicas, yields, varieties and pests. It seemed a shame to ruin it and the Consultant nearly didn't. As they fell into another reflectory silence watching as a cabbage white floated over like a Dornier bomber, he nearly thought that this was asking too much. There were risks, it was a lot to ask, it wasn't going to be easy. He didn't want another friend, or himself to enter a long stretch. He could find someone else, but he really valued his friend's skill. It would be more difficult without him.

"I get that trouble at our age is to be avoided. I get that time is more precious now but there is a guy I would like you to meet. He is good with locks but doesn't know safes. You could mentor him and let him take the risks with you as his consultant. You would have nothing to lose from meeting him and you are always good company at a card table. And if this job is of interest then you will know the team and have the final say of how we play this. It will be up to you to be in, or out. And to be honest with you, I am still thinking on if we do it or not, so your professional view would be good. On the bit that interests you, I know that it is physically a big unit." Tom canted his head at that and looked quizzical.

"Fridge-freezer big?" the Consultant nodded with certainty. "Do you know the best thing about big safes?" he carried on before there was an answer "they have lots of stuff in them. I have not cracked a big safe for years. In the past they have held lots of ready cash." Tom flicked the last of the thermos after the butterfly, in an absent gesture and exhaled. His interest was piqued. "So, what is the job?" The die was cast. That was a buying sign, he was interested. He needed the money and wanted the adventure. When you are good at something you want to do it. He was good at cracking safes, he wanted to do it.

"Do you know, I am not too sure what it is. Is that going to be a problem?" Tom rubbed his chin and gently snorted.

"That's the way it always is! It's always Schrodinger's cat. That's the fun of it. You never know what's in it till it's open."

"Come for a card's night and you can hear what details I have and make a decision from there."

"Well one decision is known."

"What's that?"

"Don't tell my wife."

8

"Can I have a copy of that?" The Consultant was in a locksmiths, like anyone else who popped in for a key to be cut. His gloved hand passed over a key. They were both aware of the CCTV and that it had no audio. The shop assistant looked at the key like it was made of gold and gently leaned back on his workbench in a relaxed style.

"It's good to see you. It's been a while, thought you had forgotten me."

'Why does everyone say that', thought the Consultant. "How can I forget a man of your talents."

"Well, there is forgetting, there's not needing and then there's using someone else." The Consultant got the barb in that comment. He stretched out his hand asking for the key back.

"Don't be hasty, just saying I like to be appreciated,

this relationship is all a bit one-way." An ego needed nurturing. Locksmiths are easy to find. You just need a phone book, but one that could do what this job required was not so easy. And locksmiths with negotiable morals are rare, a locksmith caught in a burglary tends to limit future career opportunities.

"I'm in need of a key, I have lost the original but have an impression and there are a few more that you might need to look at, a site visit if you will. Bit of variation, not an easy task, working under pressure. Needs a certain skill set. You'd be good at it." This wasn't going to be difficult. The locksmith had been right when he said that he'd not had any jobs from the Consultant recently. He would take the bait.

"Yeah I can look into that" and he handed the key back after wiping it in an oily cloth.

"Good news. Come to a card's night and you can give me the estimate then."

9

The castellation theory of protection predates castles themselves. From time immemorial people who wanted protection would have defences of various types in concentric rings about themselves. The Consultant was no different in planning in hard defences over the years. Counter surveillance had changed over time and he had factored that in and he became more cautious and reclusive. His first line of defence was to move to an enclosed location on the Wolds. A substantial old farmhouse, double fronted, Cotswold stone, various outbuildings but remote. A long driveway led to a court at the front of the house and it had a low-walled garden at the rear. It had good lines of sight in most directions and when the

Consultant walked his boundaries he looked for some distance to the cover and obstacles that others could hide behind. The other land around was farmed, rented to neighbours for sheep and crops. But behind his barn there was some open ground and then woodland. This was not too far away and that was a useful resource as it provided cover and seclusion away from the house that the Consultant could use. He had secreted things within the wood that he would never want found on his property or within his possession.

Glazier arrived first as he needed to pass the internal security checks. If he failed these checks then there was time to turn the other guests away. His arrival on the driveway created a real and metaphorical buzz and the Consultant checked his CCTV and then walking outside to meet him. Whilst this was, and looked friendly, it also meant that the Consultant put distance between his house and Glazier. They exchanged pleasantries on "found it OK" and then the Consultant got to business.

"So, I hope that you know that I trust you and I will vouch for you today, but if we are going to talk frankly, as a group, everyone needs to trust everyone and they do not know you. So everyone gets checked on the way in. We all get checked." The Consultant nodded with wide eyes at Glazier to emphasise that there were no exceptions. "So can you open the back?" and the rear doors of the Transit van were pointed to.

There was no prevarication or obstruction, Glazier seemed to get it, or to be submissive, either-way, he just walked up and opened both the doors so that the Consultant could see exactly the space that he himself had hidden in.

"Follow me. There are lockers in the porch for your phone, keys, wallet change and anything else in your pockets. Come in empty handed. And shoes off, there are some slippers to use. The first bit is to save prison time and the second bit is to save my carpets." The enclosed porch projected from the face of the house and was the space to kick off muddy wellies and hang a wet Barbour. There was a long bench, storage and small individual lockers for your personal bits and bobs. The Consultant stood at the entrance to the house proper with a pair of those cheap, thin, hotel slippers that he handed over at the opportune time.

"OK, next bit." The consultant went through the front door into the hallway and turned and beckoned Glazier through.

"This feels like I am at an airport scanner."

"That's, because it is an airport scanner." Glazier stepped through and turned and saw a green glow around the architrave of the door.

"Cool isn't it. As I said everyone is checked" and the Consultant stepped into and out of the porch himself and Glazier could see the green glow again. The Consultant gave the internationally recognised sign to show that he planned to frisk Glazier and then they got onto that task.

"Where did you get an airport scanner?"

"The are made down the road in Cleeve and I have a contact who was able to get the parts and who liked a challenge. I mean, who wants an *actual* airport scanner in their hallway; so we planned this out and got it installed. I don't trust everyone I let into my house and this has been literally disarming in the past." Glazier pondered who he was getting involved with, this guy who was very busy patting him down, seemed pleasant, direct sometimes, but also friendly at times. Yet people came to his home with guns. Was he getting out of his depth here…if he was then perhaps the point of no return was coming up soon.

"So how many more are coming tonight?"

"Just two more. Come through and help yourself

to a drink, all I'd like you to do is let them know what you know, I will fill in some details and then they will ask questions and we will come to a decision on who wants in. Between you and I, it is the older guy that you will meet that we need, he would be nigh-on impossible to replace. But let's see how it goes." They had moved into an adjacent room and sat at a good-sized table covered in a green baize cloth. Coasters and a pack of cards made it into a card table. There were two empty seats and an air of anticipation. They made small talk on the views on the drive out, the house, the cold weather and then the buzzer sounded and the Consultant left to frisk the next arrival.

Glazier's nerves got the better of him and he stalked the room. It was an impressive room, clearly the dining room. Oak panelled with a large marble fireplace with a good fire within, Georgian windows that were shuttered. Privacy and warmth. He suspected this room ran the length of the house. It held the door they entered through and another in the same wall, past the fireplace that he suspected would go into the central hallway. It was large enough for sofas to be set by the fireplace and for the card table without any squeeze. He backed towards the fireplace and warmed his arse and looked out towards the closed shuttered windows and thought that his trousers may catch fire. The door opened and a young, tall guy entered, good build but he had a bit of a belly but the best thing he had was a smile and hand offered. Glazier didn't think he was in trouble with this guy.

"And this is Glazier, the introductions are one-way till we know who wants in, there is one more to go and then we will get going." And it was not long before they did get going. Tom was the last man ushered in and he offered a hand to both of them in-turn and whilst friendly it was less enthusiastic. The kind of smile you would offer your proctologist prior to an exam. They were pointed to their seats had soft drinks and tea provided and got down to business.

"Thanks for coming. This is a proposal that has come from Glazier here" there was a waft of the hand to the Consultant's right "and I have been looking at the potentiality of it and you can both contribute if you wish" there was a waft of the hand to his left on the *both*. "As Glazier has not been here before I can let you know that I have checked out what I can on him. His personal story holds water and he has been recommended to me by a mutual friend (a name was shared that one person nodded at) and I have checked that out as best I can. I have, clearly, found no issues. So, to the job at hand. Again, for the new boy, we will be circumspect on some details at this juncture but we will share what we know, then everyone can ask questions and then take a check on who wants in." He looked to his right and left with a warm smile, as if he was inviting them for a weekend away, the old guy smiled back with a look of someone who expected a timeshare hard-sell on this weekend away. "So Glazier, take them through what you told me." The telling was slow and deliberate after some initial nerves and with the Consultant nudging for more detail here and there. The other two remained quiet.

"And there you have it in a nutshell" offered the Consultant to round off the exposition "I have a plan to get the four of us into the place and for the CCTV. Where you two come in are the series of doors and then the safe to overcome. Let's do the doors first, Glazier has an imprint of the first." The Consultant offered his hand to Glazier and then passed the imprint to the younger man on his left. He opened the small tin that had been passed and he studied the content, turning the blu tack block so that it caught the light. "Any problems?"

"No" the younger man shook his head gently as he

said that and placed the block in front of himself. "It's a quality lock but I have the blanks and can cut it from that" he pointed to the block "and it's a good impression, so I would have a good chance of getting it right first time. No guarantee though, cutting from a key is more accurate, but we should be good."

"And what do you think of the other doors that have been described?"

"Well. The iron gate sounds easy I wouldn't think that will have a sophisticated lock, so I could pick that soon enough but we don't seem to know much of the last one. If it is the same as the first then I will have my work cut out to pick that, but I would expect it done in thirty minutes or less."

The Consultant nodded as if he knew if that was a good prognosis or not (he didn't have a clue) and then shifted his gaze to Tom and asked for his thoughts on the safe.

"May I?" he said to the man sat next to him and gestured to the blu tack block. This seemed to non-plus the younger guy, but he soon got the message.

"Oh, yes sure" and he passed the tin and block. The older man breathed out heavily and also examined it with a professional eye. "What blank would you use?" he asked and the younger man responded, there was some nodding from the older man who then asked more technical questions on locks. This instantly went over the Consultant's head but he enjoyed the two experts discussing the doors and locks. They seemed to get to a mutually agreed end of the questions and answers. All the questions from the older man had been answered by the younger, it had been an examination and the young man was not sure why; but then it became clear when the older man moved his full attention back to Glazier and asked "tell me about the safe?" There were detailed questions again, but it was clear that there wasn't too much detail available. The Consultant stepped into a growing pause.

"What are your thoughts on the safe and locks?" the old man pulled a face, ran a hand through his hair and then put his elbows on the table and laced his fingers together. "Well. The guy to my left knows his locks and once you have got us inside this place he can get through the doors. He will have to be very good to get the first door open first time with the impression. As he has pointed out they do have quality locks and the last one is an unknown but I suspect he is being modest with an estimate for thirty minutes." They exchanged sideways nods to acknowledge and accept the flattery "and then we have the safe. We don't have much to go on, but two dials have been mentioned. The best safes are put in when the buildings are built. What do we know on that?" The Consultant had a small moleskin notebook on the table and as he referred to that he stated that the building had always had the same owner and on finding the detail he wanted he stated the year built.

"Good. That fits. OK so there is a German safe manufacturer who came up with a great way to increase security on their already well built and secure safes. But it only worked on big safes as they put two doors on those. Each had a lock of its very own and both had to be unlocked to allow the doors to swing open" and on that he lifted his hands from the baize to mimic opening a cupboard or wardrobe, swinging two doors open simultaneously. "You can have the same or different combinations on both locks. They are relatively easy to crack, but should both combinations differ then it takes twice the time. And they are good locks to start with. If we are lucky two hours. An hour each. Four hours each or perhaps more as an outside guess. But the good news would be that these went out of fashion quickly. They were big, expensive and time-locks were on the horizon so things moved on. I can get into it given time."

A pause grew again, it seemed that everyone had said their piece and the Consultant took charge and looked at the three in front of him and nodded in their direction as he stated the facts.

"OK, so we know that Glazier has these packages and where he delivers them. I have checked out that there is no gang connection, drugs or explosives, but what is actually going on remains a mystery to me. We can get through the internal doors in a reasonable time and the safe can be cracked; given time. Glazier is in as it's his plan. I am happy to front the funds and settle a plan that suits on how we all get in. I myself am prepared to go in. And the locks and safe can be overcome with the right expertise. So are you two in?"

The younger player looked to his right but didn't wait for a response in that direction "but this guy knows locks *and* safes, what do you need me for?"

"Ah" the older man started in a rather sheepish tone, "I had a brush with the law and had to clear out my rather lovely workshop and all my blanks are gone. I have very little hardware and tools left. I had to convince the plod, and my wife, that I had retired for good. I still have the knowledge in my head to get into that safe, but I am not going to go anywhere equipped to steal. With another locksmith on the job then I have deniability and you bring all the tools. But, to be frank, I don't want to get caught at all. So, this job would have to be good for me to want to leave my retirement." He lifted his gaze from the baize and fixed the Consultant with a quizzical gaze. "You want us all to do this without knowing what we are stealing?"

The Consultant sat back in his chair and exhaled. That was the elephant in the room. He still did not know what was in the packages.

"I don't know what is in them. I know it's small, portable and valuable. It's keeping a growing family business going for some years. All I can say is that my 20% off the top is for a reason. I can finance and arrange the plan, cover contingencies and legal costs, should they arise and fence the stuff. You will get a quarter share as clean cash into offshore accounts. I would hope that I can easily move whatever it is and monetise our hard work and do that quickly…that is the way I work. Some of you have seen that before. That is what I am bringing to the table. I don't know what we are stealing…but we don't want 'stuff' we want clean cash. Leave that aspect to me to worry about." Glazier raised the next point, with some trepidation, but they all took their hat off to him for saying it.

"But there may be nothing of value?"

"That's the risk I take by funding things up-front…and perhaps you too, depending on what worthless things we find in the safe. But yes, as with any such job, we may walk away with nothing." Tom was the next to make a point.

"And if we get caught, I don't get to see my grandchildren again." It wasn't a question. A statement. Glazier swallowed, they needed the old guy and he did not seem to have been won over. He looked at the Consultant who then lifted his head and addressed the oldest man at the table.

"First up there are the normal precautions that I take. No-one knows what we are planning but us. There are no eyes and ears on this but our own and that is the way it stays. We do not talk to anyone about this but those in this room ever. Ever. If we get caught outside then my legal man will be all over it. If we are all inside then there are two of you who can cover the locks and safe. We will stand a story up that you were there but nothing to do with us. He is the safe man." And as the Consultant said this he pointed to the younger guy. "My lawyer will suggest that you are the safe cracker and he" and with that there was a point to Tom, "has no connection to this at all. My lawyer will jump up and down to get you released and we will all need to agree to do that as we have no-one else to get into the safe. Opening the safe is the key part. And for your compliance on this, to potentially take a bigger fall than you need to, he will take you under his wing as an apprentice if you like. You know locks and he knows safes. This is succession planning. If you do well he will continue to train you up, hand on the baton and I get to have a new safe man. It isn't pretty. But it's the last resort if we do get caught inside. If that is the eventuality then leave it to my legal guy. Say nothing to anybody but your lawyer; but that's the plan I propose for that end point."

Silence fell and the older and younger guy pondered. Risk and reward for both of them, this proposal did reduce the risk for the elder and he knew the legal eagle the Consultant used. He would be in good hands.

"So hands up if you are in." said the Consultant raising his right hand at the elbow so that his palm was level with his head. Clear and unequivocal. Glazier was, of course, next and raised his hand slightly higher in a sub-conscious demonstration that he really wanted this to work for him. Then the younger man with a faux sign of resignation, but the Consultant knew he really wanted this to work too. He really wanted more from life and wanted the cash to make that happen. And they all looked to the elder to decide and, as if a lock opened he suddenly decided and raised his hand in a swift affirmation. The Consultant was pleased and relieved.

"OK! Everyone is allowed to change their minds so share any worries so that we get the plan tight and right, but we have a good team and I will crank up the planning. Glazier I want to *formally* introduce you to Lock and Safe."

10

The evening then did progress onto cards and a few drinks and it was only a few. Beds were offered if people wanted more to drink as no-one should be pulled for being over the limit and end up in the cells being asked questions on where they had spent this evening. So these tough, hardened crims had squash and tea. They enjoyed the cards and would be able to state without word of a lie that they had all met to play cards and also be able to know who, won what, who was jammy and who may have been cheating. Plus, they got to know one-another. The two locksmiths being placed in this space was a plan to see if they could work together and they got on like a house on fire. They were used to working independently and when on these nefarious tasks they had no-one to refer or discuss things with, they seemed pleased with an outlet to discuss issues and learns. The Consultant was very pleased with the provision of this network, he would benefit from a new safe man but he could also see that his old friend would have a retirement plan; he could now act as a consultant to this protégé, handing him work as well as tips. All taking their appropriate cuts. And on this job he had the man that he needed. Now all he had to do was to work on getting them all in and out of the offices. The night had gone well. The fact that they still did not know what they were stealing seemed to be a minor irritant. But the Consultant was finding that scratching this itch was becoming painful.

11

There was a list of manufacturers that he worked with, spreading tasks amongst them, not relying on one but also trying not to forget the good ones. Why he turned to Luke for this job wasn't obvious outside of this rotation through his contacts, but he wanted a toolbox and remembered that Luke worked on cars and had many such toolboxes. He dropped by unannounced. This was a suburban semi in a nice part of Gloucester, good sized houses in a good size garden and a minor road off a minor road. Looming above it was the green expanse of Chosen Hill. An outlier of the Cotswold escarpment that bookended this part of Gloucestershire and separated the Wold from valley. You could see the other book end in the form of May Hill that marked the nearly Welsh side of the valley. And it you looked out of the right windows in this suburb you could see a far-off view of the Malvern Hills. All-in-all a nice quiet spot. He walked the short drive and had to step onto the slightly shabby lawn to navigate the very battered Fiesta being worked on. Short legs poked from the bonnet and the Consultant was surprised to see a young girl, around twelve perhaps, deep into the carburettor. At the look of her hands she had been bathed in engine oil. She looked surprised to see him and shuffled backwards to get her feet on the ground as her legs were too short to stand over the valence and reach the engine.

"Is your dad in?" was responded to with a nod and through walking away past another car and into the workshop. That second car had roll cage, dented panels and graphics and conveyed the racing credentials of the owner and his mechanical abilities. The graphic was a large roadrunner that matched the flanks of the car and seemed animated itself.

They entered the garage area and it was a deceptively large workshop, well organised and spreading further back into the garden. A larger space than the garage doors implied. It was warm and had the sweet smell of hot, clean, oils. It was bright, clean and was dominated by a milling machine, lathe and central workbench, at which a tall, slender man was working with a file. He instinctively reached out to shake hands then retracted the hand and removed vinyl gloves and tried again.

"Good to see you, I thought you had forgotten me." It had been over a year since the Consultant had used these services on another task.

"Well, I was waiting for a job that needed your skills, and here I am" and an expansive gesture was used as the Consultant looked around the room like it was the first time and continued "you're looking thin. I noticed the For Sale sign and why isn't your daughter in school. Is everything alright?"

"Ah." The word hung in the air and the mechanic leaned forward onto the work bench, letting his weight fall onto his locked arms in a dejected manner that reflected on the inflection used in the word 'Ah'. He shook his head slightly and stated matter-of-factly "my wife died. Eight months ago and we are off to family in the North. I'm trying to find a buyer and she will move schools soon; and to be frank, she can learn more from me at the moment. She is great mechanically and at art. She paints all the cars, we take commissions" and with that he shooed her outside. "No offers on the house yet so I can pick up work, if there is some going?"

The guy was semi-legitimate (everyone preferred cash-in-hand, that was a given) and knew that the Consultant wasn't someone you found in the yellow pages. He would be expecting an esoteric and challenging job and that the real purpose of some tasks were hidden.

"This is what I need" stated the Consultant spreading some photos on the table of a red, tool chest that was on wheels and was the type with lots of draws for lots of spanners, "I want it to look just like the one in the photos, same size, same patina, the same wear and dirt but I

38

want the front to be false, no drawers, it's a door. Nothing inside, no shelf. It should be lockable from inside and out." The slender guy looked at the photos and went over each one several times.

"Do you want the hinges on the left or right?"

"Whatever is easier for you."

"Are you in a rush?"

"No. How is two weeks?"

"That should be fine. I recognise the brand" he waved a hand behind himself, "mine are similar but I can get this brand quickly enough and make the required changes and then make it look old. How's two grand?"

The Consultant did not flinch but thought the price high. But this was a negotiation and they had a starting point and so he made a counteroffer, "a grand cash for your time plus whatever you pay for the tool chest", he offered his hand and it was shaken. He was glad as he didn't want to start chaffering over the cost, as this was the man for this job.

"OK I will let you know when it is ready, but within two weeks. Do you have a number?"

"No. I will just be back with the cash two weeks today. And if anybody ever asks, this is a cabinet to put my pillar drill into, for safe keeping."

That didn't make much sense, but it was a cover that they could both use if they were asked to explain why this was being constructed. And the transaction was done, there was a final handshake and consolation for the bereavement, not that the Consultant had ever known the lady, but it felt the right thing to do and they had a short conversation on early, lingering deaths and he left, seeing himself out.

The girl was stood with the carburettor in hand, inspecting its innards, petrol fumes hung in the air and she brushed hair back smearing oil over her forehead as he passed.

"You should be in school" he said half seriously with a wagging finger as he strolled past.

12

In the intervening two weeks the Consultant tried to scratch the itch. The itch on what they could be stealing. He didn't want to ask too many people too many questions. Glazier had suggested he ask his new best friend, the security guy at the firm, what he knew; but that could be something that would draw attention. The Consultant had learned in the past that the times of really difficult decisions are rare. Often you know what you need to do, you are just reluctant to do it. In this case he knew he just had to stakeout the Mercedes driving brothers and see what he could find. It was as frustrating as he expected. Many hours spent learning nothing and some pounds expended on trips that returned no benefit. He had followed both 'brothers' (as he now assumed that was the case) to their homes and tried to spot a routine, but they seemed to freestyle when they were in the office and away.

On two consecutive mornings he followed one to Birmingham airport and then lost contact at the car drop-off and the other to London. The second tail looked more promising at times and was technically easier in the mele of bodies in train and tube stations. Especially when the brother stepped out of the train at Paddington and turned left and headed away from the Circle line and onto the less travelled Hammersmith and City. They jumped off at Euston Square and took a leisurely but direct route through Bloomsbury. This was looking promising until a few turns took them to the first skyscraper built in London, the Centre Point building. The brother walked in and was too quick through reception for the Consultant to catch up and catch what was said. He was asked 'How can I help' by one of the receptionists and considered bluffing through the security, but took a swerve away and tried to catch what floor the brother took in the lift. He couldn't see from the remoteness of the turnstiles that separated those in and those out. He didn't linger, just exited onto New Oxford Street and studied the list of businesses listed with offices at Centre Point. It was a very long list of anodyne names. He took a coffee and waited. Perhaps the brother would go for lunch with his contact and that would result in information…but the Consultant had lunch on his own and saw no brother emerge. He must have eaten in as at 15:00 he did emerge and took the tube and train home. The Consultant had learned something; this was a dead end. He would have to fully realise that he would not know what they were stealing until they had the safe open. And then fence it as best he could. They would be like a teenager putting in the windows of cars to rifle through the glove boxes and central console and hope they find wallet and cash. He didn't like trusting to luck. You were not in his profession for long by trusting to luck.

And so for the rest of the two weeks he resorted to his day jobs. First was the consultancy itself. He kept up with the emails (all anonymous contacts on the dark web) and pub meetings. He knew not to do too many jobs concurrently as he always wanted to provide the right service. Turning jobs down was also a fine tactic, handing good jobs off to others, recommending 'better' options did mean that he could monitor what jobs did progress. He would automatically be suspicious of 'great jobs' that came his way that he turned away that then never materialised. It was one of his mantras that 'people are allowed to change their minds' but he knew entrapment was alive and well within the police service. Another mantra was 'trust comes with reliability' and to be reliable he knew that he had to deliver consistently. If he had too many concurrent jobs then consistency was difficult and he didn't want or need to be greedy.

His front job was scrap metal recycling. Small scale, mainly aluminium and gold. Stolen jewellery was identifiable and a lump of molten gold was not. He loved the metallurgy from his school days, back in the times of metalwork and woodwork lessons in school. He loved working in the forge, in sand-casting, the smells of gas, hot metals, wet sands, fumes, spumes of water as metal was quenched. He branched from the fence that he used to work for into the scrap side once he had his current house. He used one of the barns and bought the tools and furnace and had legitimate and not-legitimate metals alloyed and a useful front business; plus the tools, forge and furnace had other usages. So, he kept himself busy and then returned to the manufacturer as planned.

13

"I see that school's still out." The girl was painting a three-dimensional number onto the bonnet of, probably, the car that she had in parts on his last visit. She had seen him approaching and had readied herself by putting the brush down carefully and passed him a smile as she called for her dad and led the way into the workshop. The kid stood to one side then melted into the background as the two men said 'hi' and exchange pleasantries. The Consultant knew she was there but had no intention of talking about any details and did like the idea that she wanted to participate with the adult world. On the workbench was something covered in a large dust sheet and with the correct solemnity the cloth was withdrawn.

First impressions were good, the Consultant and engineer referred to the photos and walked about the workbench to take in the job, as if it were a work of art and they were critics.

"Obviously getting the right base unit was fine, changing the interior, removing the drawers to make a door wasn't challenging of itself, but getting the look right" and a gesture of grasping something ephemeral was made at this point "that was the difficult bit. I got the resident artist to help. I didn't have anything for what the back should look like so just went freestyle and aged that." The Consultant liked that unnecessary attention to detail, second impressions were good. Quality job.

"Can you show me the mechanism."

"Yes! No problem." You could sense some pride was going to be exhibited in the intonation there. "I kept the key lock. When it's locked then it is locked and nothing will happen. I used a loft-latch." He checked and saw bemusement so explained. "Ahh, when you close the door it holds. When you push the door, it springs open. These locks are used on loft doors in ceilings" and with that he pushed the front panel of the cabinet, there was a click and it swung slowly open. The manufacturer wanted a fanfare or a round of applause and he may have got one if the Consultant hadn't had a sudden revelation. The interior dimensions were small. He had foreseen that space was going to be tight inside the cabinet, perhaps uncomfortably so, but with the required interior bracing and locking mechanism space was *really* tight. There was no way he would fit in there. Damn. He swallowed and looked again. His plan was crumbling. Two weeks and a grand flushed and back to square one.

"But here's the best bit, up you get kid." The girl stepped forward and with ease placed her hands on the workbench and hopped onto the table. With one step she got to the cabinet, swivelling backwards into it and deftly lifted her feet inside. She was folded and snug but not wincing or squished. A thin arm reached for the door and pulled it in a gentle arc and it clicked into place.

"and now it's locked from the inside" her dad pushed and pulled the door and nothing happened "I have made it look like the drawers are locked, so don't leave the key in the lock as that would confuse things" he gestured at the lock "it just looks like it is locked. OK kid." There wasn't a click this time, the door just swung open and the child stepped out and stood there looking down at them both.

"So, what do you think?"

The Consultant thought that he would have to recruit a child onto his team of burglars. He tried to put the preposterous thought out of his head. But the solution to his problem stood there smiling at him. She really should have been at school.

14

The Consultant thought through the problem, he didn't like being put on the spot but he had seen this situation before. You had a problem and the solution, it's just that the solution is unpalatable so people prevaricate. He liked to ponder problems that offered options, but he knew what had to be done.

"Can you unlock the boot of my car, ready to put this in?" The Consultant stated that whilst offering his keys up to the girl and nodding to the doorway. She glanced at her father who acquiesced, took the keys and jumped down and left.

"It's a Trojan Horse."

The kid's father looked non-plussed, you could see him trying to examine and explain the words. The Consultant gestured at the cabinet, gathered his thoughts and realised that his starting point had not been great, yet he repeated the words whilst the kid's father looked baffled.

"It's a Trojan Horse. The plan is to place this in a workshop to replace one that looks identical to it, the one in the photos. No-one will notice the change. And then, when everyone has left the workshop someone can get out of it and open a door so that others can get into that workshop. I had planned to be inside this…but I can now see that I am not going to fit." The engineer looked into the open cabinet as if it were a problem he could fix.

"Well, I can't take the bracing out without weakening it, I didn't know you wanted that." There was concern in his voice, he thought that some fault was being found.

"It's just too tight, but your kid could be able to do the job. They would be in there for around an hour. Long enough to let the workshop close and then they can get out and wait for a signal to unlock the external door." Silence. Both men looked at each other and then at the cabinet, sitting there with the door wide open, showing the space within.

"What's in it for me?" A telling question thought the Consultant. Not 'is it dangerous' or 'what's the risk of being caught'. The answer to the question that was asked was clear, everyone involved took a share or get paid a flat fee for a given task. But he could see that those with a fee often got greedy if they found out what the take was. With this role, they wouldn't know what the take was; and he didn't want to keep paying out when he had no idea if he was going to make anything out of this job. "It's a fifth share of the profit from the job and before you ask, I don't know what that could amount to." He felt that he would need to encourage this ask over the line so continued "you've been paid for your works so are on top of this at the moment, we are not asking for much now. If it goes pear shaped then legal services are provided and everyone says nothing. As a minor your kid will be fine. You just need to agree a story of why she is in Cheltenham at night. Got on the wrong bus or something. Everyone on my jobs says nothing so she has nothing to fear there. She will be OK with that?" There was a nod in response. "And we don't know what the job entails yet, there is uncertainty that I don't want to explain to you. But you get a fifth share of whatever profit there is. So there's very little risk and potential for a good upside and all for an evening's work. Your house is for sale and you plan to move, so this could work out well for everyone concerned."

Silence again as the other man took up that position again of leaning forward with straight arms on the workbench, there was some dejection in his demeanour, resignation that it had come to this, he had led his daughter into a life of crime; if his wife was still alive he wouldn't even be having this conversation. But she was dead. He was alone. Nothing was as it should be and he deserved a break, this seemed to be a gift horse. He looked into the depths of the cabinet and asked "when?"

15

They gathered at the Consultant's house for the final briefing and to make an initial 'go' or 'no-go' decision. Most of his jobs came together in a phased manner and he knew who was on-board, but this job had always been different so the Consultant was clear from the outset that those at the table could say 'no' and back out; and that would be it, the job would be off. A sigh of relief and back to the day-job. He looked around the table and made eye contact with Safe, Glazier and Lock and prepared the path ahead.

"So, this is the plan. The next time Glazier

receives a package to deliver I will circulate a message via text and we will know that the job is on the next day, so be prepared for twenty-four-hour notice. If you all respond then I will message again and we will be on. Glazier and I will meet and take the toolbox…" it was there in the dining room with them sat rather incongruously beside the sofa and the Consultant gestured at it as he spoke "…to the location not long before they are due to close. The van blocks the camera's view of the toolbox that is in the loading bay. Glazier will drop off the package as normal and that will distract the guard. I swap the toolboxes. This one is a Trojan Horse and a kid will be inside it." There were a few raised eyebrows at that but the Consultant raised a placatory hand and continued. "I will come back to that bit, but the key element is that Glazier and I then leave and we wait for the place to close up and go quiet. In the evening, I collect you all from designated locations and we head to the location again. I use a radio to make contact and the kid inside the toolbox steps out and opens the fire door at the front of the building; here." At this point a jab was made to a sketch plan. "The alarm may sound but it will go silent when the door closes. I checked the make and model and it's old tech, but we can expect it to connect to a central control and raise the alarm there. Could be patched to the police. So the key for us will be to be ready for when the fire door opens. We will be in and close the door in seconds. If the alarm is raised at a remote centre or is linked to the local police then we can expect it to be seen as a glitch, if it even gets noticed at all. But to be sure I will sort the CCTV first thing so that the kid being there and our entry is wiped. The kid will go outside as we come in and be our first look out. We will monitor police radio. If there are any issues, for example if the alarm keeps sounding or the police respond to any alarm that is raised with them then we will hear it on the radio and leave straight away. Worst case could be the police turn up really quickly and find us in the car park." There was pause for effect. "But if the coast is clear then Lock will use the replica key on the first door. He will pick the second and third doors. We will then be in the room with the safe and Safe will get to work. We will have all night, but we won't hang about. Clear up after yourself and others. We will be in Tyvek suits and wipe everything down as we go. Lock will carry all the tools and make sure that they are wiped clean before we go in. I will bin and burn everything after. Once the safe is open we will have a look at what we have, package it up and leave. Similar drill on the way out and get through the fire door quickly, but we will take the fake toolbox out with us and put the original back in its place. I then drop you all at the designated spots. You can then decide what to do as we will have an idea of the take at that time, but my expectation will be that I launder any cash, take out the expenses and fees and share the rest five ways into offshore accounts." Safe looked prepared to raise something but the Consultant cut him off politely "and let me cover that off now. I didn't want to get anyone else in on this, I was going to be inside the Trojan Horse, but look at it…it's much too snug for me to be in there any length of time so I needed to bring in someone else. I had to do it quick and didn't want to be shopping around looking for a dwarf, jockey or some unknown teenager…so I used the kid who already knew about the toolbox. They get a share; you know that's the way it goes and we all know it may be a share of nothing." He stopped talking and let the dust settle and he knew that it would be the elder statesman of the group who would speak up.

"So, we have some kid that we don't know involved. Are they going to be up to it, can they keep quiet, can they be trusted?"

"Well, I believe they can be trusted, I have worked

with her dad before and he has been fine in the past, but I have only used him to make things for me. He hasn't been involved in jobs other than that. He doesn't know what we are doing and I want to keep him in the dark. But the kid seems sound. And they are a kid, they have been told to keep quiet and my barrister will get them out if there is any trouble. But are they up to the job, can they stay in there undetected for an extended period…?" the Consultant swung around and all their eyes swivelled onto the toolbox standing close to the centre of the room. "You can come out now" and without a sound the door swung open and the kid stepped out and stood amongst them. "She's been in there" and at this point the Consultant checked his watch "nearly three hours." They all looked as she took off her headphones. "How was it?"

"Dull."

"I will get you a Gameboy." He turned back to the table "but I didn't hear a sound and she's been sitting there all the time we have been here. She is going to be up to it." The Consultant swung back to look at the kid again. "Can we all trust you to keep all that we do a secret? Can we trust you to tell no-one, not even your dad, what you see and hear, because we all need to trust each other you see? We all…" and at this the Consultant gestured to the group of men who were staring at her, "…must trust you and you need to trust us. Is that understood?"

She didn't shuffle, look away or delay.

"Yes. You can trust me. Everything is a secret. And I get a Gameboy."

Safe chuckled at that. It broke the tension. "Well, she has a small part to play. I take it that once the kid opens the fire door then they stay in the car and wait for us?"

"Yep our look-out. That and opening the door is the extent of her role but they will be with us for the getaway. But I am not planning on that being a car chase from the movies that's more to do with giving her a lift home."

Silence then fell, the firewood moving in the grate was the only sound as the Consultant looked about the table and waited for any questions and then prompted one himself. "So, what do you all think. We have our way into the place. Is it a go?" They all looked at one-another and then nodded consent and said 'yes'. The consultant turned once again to the kid.

"So, this will be the Kid. Kid meet, Mr Lock, Mr Safe and Mr Glazier and you can call me the Consultant."

16

Then they waited. There were some things that each specialist needed to arrange and the consultant had other things to gather and check. He maintained spreadsheets of checklists and accounts to ensure that everything was organised, in-place and accounted for. And that included the car for the job. It was a late model Range Rover that had plenty of room, some luxury but also no provenance or regular plates. It would disappear after the job but was too good to crush. The toolbox was ready in the boot. Gameboy and fresh batteries within it and ready. Headphones plugged into the jack to ensure it made no sound. Some biscuits in cling film (no rustling) too. The kid was in school. The Consultant had instructed her and her father that being in school would give better cover than playing truant.

And then the call came. Glazier had the package. His final one to drop off. He came around to pass on the news, which was fine with the Consultant, they put the package in the middle of the kitchen table and had tea and talked about football to defuse the excitement (or anxiety) and then waited for the responses to the password *Paris* via text. Lock was first with *Helen*. So he was OK. Safe was next with the same word about an hour later. Glazier and the Consultant both convinced themselves that they would need to wait for the Kid to leave school and be told that it was on…but both felt that her dad could just respond on his own volition with his unilateral decision. *Cassandra* was the word they didn't want to see, that would be the key word for "no-go" for this package and the plan would then be that they would scratch until the next. The two around the kitchen table chatted and regularly glanced at the phone, checking to ensure they had not missed the message's arrival. As if. And then the phone buzzed and rattled upon the table. *Helen*.

The Consultant surprised himself by gulping at the word. He exhaled. Another bridge crossed, if someone had said 'no' then he would have been relieved, but Glazier looked excited. It could have been faux, but it seemed genuine. He wanted this; a big job that took lots of issues away and took him to somewhere else. For the Consultant it was another job, but this excitement was infectious.

"We had better get ready." He reached out his hand, he wasn't sure why, perhaps he just wanted some physical contact. Glazier smiled broadly, his eyes were alive with the possibilities, it was like he had been given the keys to his first car, been handed the first present at Christmas, he was beaming. e took and shook the offered hand.

Part II – Implementation

17

The Kid was collected and they had a rendezvous with Glazier and his van in a spot away from any cameras to conduct the first stage of their plan. Whilst there wasn't too much time between school hours and office hours they were in no rush as the earlier they arrived the longer Kid would need to stay in the toolbox, but they had tried to be thoughtful and had room for padding, food and entertainment. The men had pre-arranged to be up-beat, encouraging and not to ask questions that could chip away any confidence, such as 'so do you remember what you need to do?' Both stole sideways glimpses as Kid sat with clenched fists staring straight ahead. They were all nervous. The Consultant gave some advice. Unclench your hands, open your palms, place your hands palm up on your lap and try to relax. He took his own advice and did the same breathing slowly and tried to relax.

This first stage seemed simple but held some great risk. They could be caught red-handed but were prepared to walk away smartly and Glazier would look as bemused as the others and pass it off as someone trying to steal something from his van. The Consultant judged it to be low risk though. He may not have tried otherwise. Speed and silence were key and this is how it played out.

Glazier pulled up in his now normal spot within the loading bay, opened the sliding door wide and pulled out a bucket and engaged the friendly security guard in banter and the pair headed into the kitchen area for warm, soapy water and perhaps a tea. As their voices faded and became muffled by entering the corridor the Consultant emerged from the shadow of the van and checked via the windscreen, mirrors and doorway that the coast was clear.

He lifted the toolbox from the van's bed and took a few shuffled steps to the twin toolbox. He set the Trojan Horse down but didn't wait to admire the similarity, or otherwise, it was close enough. The older toolbox's paint had faded, it had more patina. The photographs had knocked away some of the blemishes and not caught its true colours...as anyone who has dated on-line knows; pictures can be flattering. Now wasn't the time to ponder and he went to pick up the "old" toolbox and felt the weight...then rolled it towards the van and was able to heft it into the back with a slight rattle and thump. He pushed the box into the back of the van, deep into the shadows and threw a blanket over it. He was about to return to help the Kid but saw that she was manoeuvring the Trojan Horse into exactly the right place and then she had a final check, opened the door, swung in backwards and pulled her feet in. Click. It was done and nothing more was needed. There was nothing more that the Consultant needed to do. Delegation to the person best suited to the task. Sure there were some scuff marks in the dust, but the replacement was not out of place, so the Consultant stayed in the van. He just withdrew deeper into the shadows and waited for the windows to be cleaned and they departed with a cheery wave from the window by Glazier.

"All done?" said Glazier over his shoulder after a few yards.

"Yep, no issues" came a disembodied voice "and drive carefully as this toolbox weighs more than I thought and is rolling about back here."

"It all looked perfect to me, I couldn't see any change. Stage one done!"

18

One-by-one the Consultant picked up the crew from select locations away from prying eyes. He double checked with everyone, no ID and no phones, but they *had* brought what they needed and had gloves on. And then they drove to check for no tails and sat waiting looking out over the lights of Cheltenham. It was a typical autumnal night, the dark nights had drawn in early and had drawn in the cold nights too. They all knew this would be a difficult time to be arrested as they were equipped to steal, but their checklist of things to do included wiping everything down to remove their own fingerprints. A 'going equipped' charge would have to apply to all of them and there would be plenty of doubt sown and lots of reminders that everyone would be innocent unless proven guilty. Most innocent of all would be the convicted safe cracker with a bag of safe cracking tools, but that would be where Lock came in to muddy the waters. Whilst Lock had no convictions were the tools due to his legitimate trade? English law protects us all and a good lawyer is essential protection if you are playing outside the law. So they sat with the boot containing their tools and equipment, with their own pockets empty and in a relaxed mood. The stolen toolbox was also in the boot, but that didn't have their prints on and would only muddy waters further as it was more tools with no claiming owner. Unless its theft was noticed and linked to them. Having the stolen toolbox was a risk worth taking. Things are only stolen if the owner says so and he expected the owner not to miss this toolbox. Whilst the Consultant had brought a Range Rover (now sharing its number plate with one currently for sale at a local dealer) for speed, versatility and durability it was also spacious and well heated so they sat happily chatting and working through footy, tele, films and were getting to 'what they would do with the money' when the ignition was turned and the Consultant said not to 'count chickens'.

A small cheer went up as they rolled off Cleeve Hill and headed into town and looked down on the lights of Cheltenham, Gloucester, Tewkesbury plotting a shimmering path through the Severn valley. It was a clear night and other cars' lights loomed large in the mirrors that were assiduously checked and they eventually passed by the target. They drove straight past with the Consultant watching the road and all the others scanning the property and both sides of the road for anything out of place. They drove around the block and came back into the car park and reversed to the fire door and turned off and waited.

This was the time for them to pull out. Was there anything amiss. Any sign. The engine plinked and ticked in the silence as they all looked into the shadows beyond the streetlights. It wasn't late in the night, people were driving and were about. They didn't want to wait too long themselves. Everyone was happy and so now was the time. The Consultant made the call. He reached into the glove box and retrieved a two-way radio, he turned it on, checked the channel and keyed the mike. He didn't say anything. Just keying the mike sent silence across that frequency, if you were listening then you would hear the step change in static. And now the car full of crew listened for that same change in static. And then it came, a clear click, pause and release. All clear. The Consultant liked the dramatic pause and crackle of excitement as he swung in his seat and addressed the expectant faces.

"Gentlemen, are you ready?" He received thumbs up, smiles of bravado and nods and then they all exited the car.

They gathered at the tailgate in a well-rehearsed sequence as time was of the essence here. Each collected the items they would take in and then the boot was closed and they formed into a crocodile beside the fire door. There was a glance of affirmation between them and the Consultant knocked and then stood back.

Instantaneously several things happened. The door opened and Kid emerged. The alarm started ringing. The crocodile shuffled with some speed through the door. The fire door was closed. The alarm stopped ringing. Kid got into the back seat of the Range Rover and silence descended. Breath was held. And nothing then happened. That was good.

Miles away an alarm company didn't register that an alarm notification had appeared and been re-set.

The team were handed head torches, helped each other into their Tyvek suits and set to work.

19

Lock led Safe to the first door and took the key he had cut from a box within his small tool bag. The moment of truth.

He took the knee to get on eye level, wriggled the key into his gloved hand and slid the key into the cylinder. Everything was smooth. He applied pressure and felt it hold. It did not turn. He released. Could they have fallen at the first hurdle? Could he make a mistake that ruined everything? He swallowed and tried again. He applied the slightest jiggle and then it turned sweetly and he pushed the door open. No-one saw him close his eyes with relief. He removed the key, replaced it in its box and put that back in the tool bag and brought a wedge from the bag to hold the first door open.

"Good work" offered Safe. He knew that cutting that copy hadn't been straight-forward, it was a good lock with tight tolerances and hard-wearing materials, not the type of lock to ease over years. But from a lock that they knew they were into other realms now.

Lock and Safe surveyed the next door and Glazier followed along. This was the open gate and from the description they expected a heavy lock for strength, but nothing subtle. They both tried to take in clues from the view that they had, which was not much in the torch light. Basically, all they could see was a well-worn keyhole of some size. Lock reasoned that it was better to start than to look and took the picks from the tool bag, selected a size (large) and set to moving the pins and springs in a finger ballet of twisting and manipulating.

Lock looked over his shoulder at the smiling Safe as he anticipated the deadbolt moving out of the face plate and the gate then swung open. This too was wedged and on they went.

"So that was easy" whispered an encouraging Glazier.

"Yep. I think it was there to stop a brute force attack rather than a subtle one." Glazier looked back at the solid and broad-gauge steel frame set into the wall, but the lock was the weak link. One more door. Things were progressing well. They passed side doors that looked like they would lead to offices and one door on their right stood open to offer a view of an office, with desk, PC screen and stapler, calendar etc. and they came to the final door in the corridor.

Again Safe and Lock looked at the challenge and they didn't like what they saw. This was similar to the first lock. The gate had lulled them into thinking that the locks got easier, but that wasn't the case. Safe was aware that Lock was not looking at him, which was just as well as he had involuntarily winced when he saw the challenge. This just got a lot more difficult. He put a hand on Lock's shoulder and they both acknowledged the task at hand.

"You can do it. It's just going to take a while" and Lock nodded without taking his eyes off the task. He did start and Safe backed away and moved Glazier back too and whispered in his ear.

"Most locks have pins that move up and down and the

key is shaped to lift and drop the pins. That lock" and with this Safe poked an accusatory finger of distaste, "has pins that turn depending on the angle, the facets on the key. So he will need to move each one up *and* around. It's a fiddle, needs some tools to hold things in-place and it needs some time. So best just leave him to it."

20

On entry Consultant had headed to the office of the security guard and placed the radio he used to surveil the police on the desk. Nothing of note at all so far. He turned his attention of the CCTV video recorder. Removing the evidence of their arrival was key. He could have just taken the whole shebang and destroyed the lot, but he was cautious and there was a possibility, for example, if the key Lock had made did not work, that they would all leave and come back another day. So he wanted to cover their tracks in a subtle way. All he had had was a brief description from Glazier but that and his intuition had been enough to make a plan. He swung a large bag from his shoulder, unzipped it and took a power cable and plugged in his own VCR. He stopped the tape recording the CCTV, ejected it and pushed it into his own recorder and set it to rewind. There was a shelf with an ordered collection of regimented VHS tapes, identical but numbered. The whine from his own machine increased in pitch, the tape accelerated and with an abrupt jolt it stopped and out popped the rewound tape, the number seven on its edge.

"Lucky seven." The next tape due to be placed into the CCTV VCR by the security guard would be number eight. Its contents would be a few weeks old and were deemed to not be needed and would be videoed over. The Consultant took number eight from the shelf. His own VCR was a commercial copier, used to duplicate and record from one tape to another at speed. He inserted both tapes and set eight to be duplicated. The recording of their means of entry started to disappear.

The Consultant watched and listened to the machine start its work and pulled the walkie-talkie from the bag and asked Kid how things looked. The response was swift, "nothing. Everything is quiet out here."

"OK, well get comfortable and we will see you soon" and with that the Consultant left the recorders doing their thing and headed toward the corridor that would lead to the safe.

It was Safe himself who he came to first. He was stood at the outer door, arms folded and shifting his weight from foot to foot with nerves.

"How's it going?"

"The cut key worked a charm, the next was a strong room door, but had a weak lock and he was through that quickly. But he is now on a quality lock, I thought it best to leave him to it. He has done a good job so far so will be fine."

"The kid says it's all quiet outside and I have nothing from the police radio, so it looks like the alarm was not reported. But do you want to wait outside?" The inference here was that if the police did swoop in, it would be far better to be stood outside as an honest onlooker (albeit one that would be looked on with great suspicion) than to be found inside.

"No, no, its fine." Safe shook his head with a grimace whilst closing his eyes as he showed disdain for the suggestion. "He's got the feel for these things, I mean he's not as good as I was, but he will be through that lock in a short while and then I will get to work." He beamed a smile at that. Safe was relishing the challenge and feeling the thrill. They all were. They were well on task now, the excitement was tangible and things were still going their way.

Safe took a glance down the corridor as Lock made the final move and opened the lock and the door. Glazier was waved over and the three amigos strode down to where Lock was collecting his tools from the floor and stowing them away. He led them into the room through the now wedged open door. Safe held a torch and played it about the floor of the room. The Consultant turned off his head torch and headed over to pull all the vertical venetian window blinds and to check outside. Safe switched on an anglepoise that was on a desk close to the safe and directed its cone of light downward. Only one wall had windows and Glazier helped to close the blinds and then remained on station to check on anything moving outside. The Consultant turned and took in the room. It was a typical office space in its fluorescent lights, suspended ceiling and carpet tiles but it was devoid of plants or those pictures with mountain views containing aphorisms. It was very clean. There were five large desks, in a horseshoe, each with their own anglepoise. The desks were slightly unusual in being covered in black baize, perhaps they played a lot of solitaire? Five regulation swivel chairs were paired with each desk and against one wall, in the gap in the horseshoe was the largest safe the Consultant had ever seen. As large as a wardrobe, but perhaps slightly taller and with two doors. It was big and uniformly grey. If you got close enough it faintly smelt of oiled metal. On each door was a circular combination lock and a door handle. You could guess that you used the combination and then depressed the handle. Safe and Lock stood appraising the challenge and the Consultant took up a chair to wait the immediate review.

Safe had a good look all around, running his gloved hand over all the surfaces and explained the situation to Lock, who took a very keen professional interest.

"Clever those Germans" he held his arms out expansively, almost as an embrace, as a welcome "just look at that. They realised that some clients wanted a big safe, so they made a *big safe*. Still the same gauge of steel as a little one, just a lot more of it...so that's a heavy mother. But the expensive bit is the lock. They put on two as that makes it twice as difficult to crack. You have to open both locks to get in. You can have the same combination on each but the owners would be stupid to have the same combination twice. So all we need to do is to crack that..." and with that Safe pointed to one of the combination lock tumblers "...and then that" and he pointed to the other. He turned to Lock, "it's not overly difficult, just time consuming. I've never seen one outside of a sales brochure before. A museum piece really as the cost was high due to the duplicated locks. Later models just had the one." And with that he took the tool bag from Lock and looked about for a chair. The Consultant hastily provided the seat he was in and Safe set to work. He was an old-school cracker. He had a stethoscope and a pad of paper. Those were the tools of his trade plus hours of practice and study in the art. He closed his eyes and focused on the tick and clicks and went into a reverie and the others seemingly held their breath.

Intermittently a note would be written or be crossed out and a hushed conversation was had with Lock who was allowed to don his own stethoscope and listen in. Clearly some instruction was passed on, but then the silence and focus continued.

Eventually the Consultant went to check on Glazier, just for something to do. They both intimated the areas outside the windows that they would watch over and stood peeking out sideways, between the vertical blinds. At least the outside of the windows were clean. The road was dimly lit in the golden glow of periodic streetlamps and exterior lights, many of the house lights were now out, sensible souls were asleep. The Consultant leaned into the window to see their own car and it was the same as the whole street, misted and dark. As he had his face close to the window he felt the cold radiate from the pane and saw it cloud from his own breath.

"Is it going OK?"

"I've seen him do a safe in minutes and also to have taken hours, so difficult to say. If anyone will get in it's him. Anything outside?"

"A fox and a hedgehog."

"They are getting rare those hedgehogs."

"We should be on Autumnwatch. Is there any coffee?"

"No. No eating. No drinking. No DNA."

"I suppose having a dump is out of the question too?" The Consultant smiled but didn't feel the need to reply.

Things went quiet for a while.

"Do you have a better idea of what's in that thing?" Glazier half turned and nodded at the safe. The Consultant gestured to keep an eye outwards and stated that he didn't. He had had a good chance to look around the office and had found no clue to what may be inside the safe. He returned to the default that there had to be *something* of value to have this set-up. Surely. The Consultant looked at his watch and started to consider when they would need to leave, even if it were empty handed. He turned side onto the window and looked back towards the safe. The duo were bending to their task listening, concentrating and making minute adjustments. But then they both sat back in the same instance and Safe pushed down the handle on the left-hand door and then looked at the pair by the window and said with little emotion and in a quiet voice "halfway there. We could be lucky, just try that same combination in the right-hand lock." Lock did as instructed as Safe stood up did a turn, like an old dog looking to settle, whilst stretching his old bones. They were not surprised to find that the same combination was not used on both locks. The pair then discussed changes to the known combination in an effort to guess the numbers, they reversed the numbers used on the left, incremented them all by one, decreased them all by two and then resolved that they would need to get back down to cracking this combination too. Safe sank back into his chair, shifted his position to become comfortable, turned to a new page on his notepad and bent forward, placing his stethoscope upon the safe, closed his eyes and started all-over again.

The Consultant was getting edgy on the time it was taking and recognised that he was getting nervous and also that he shouldn't show it. He was adept at hiding his nerves. Always be calm but also always look calm. *Keep your head when all others…*he recited the poem as a distraction and then leisurely toured the building to make sure everything was as ready as possible for a quick exit, should the safe be opened. His own VCR had done its job and tape lucky seven had been rewound and placed back into the CCTV recorder, but not fully, as if it had been rewound and ejected. All of Lock's tools were in the same bag as the recorder at the door. Everything they had brought with them was ready to be taken out, even the Trojan toolbox. It didn't take long to do that tour and he returned to keep station with Glazier and waited for the safe to be cracked. Again, those at the safe both heard the last click of success and they sat up in a synchronised move of relief. The right-hand lever was depressed. After such a lengthy wait it was time for action and revelation.

Safe looked over to the window and saw both Glazier and the Consultant coming over. He waited for them to be close by and then put emphasis into these words. "This could be when the alarm goes off and the door gets kicked in. Let's see if it has been worth it."

He took hold of both handles and had to put some

effort into pulling the doors open. Those with free hands played their torches over the interior, picking up different things in their illumination, weaving their heads to peek over the other heads looking at the contents.

There were six wide shelves that looked like they could be slid out, like racks in an oven. They were as wide and deep as the large safe. The uppermost one had around twenty small velvet bags and a packet like that Glazier delivered. The next four shelves had fiddles fitted to make compartments and it seemed to be used to grade items, sorting the contents into separate piles and it could be that each shelf was also used for grading as the lowest shelf had the largest piles and then items were graduated into smaller piles on the uppermost shelf. Each member of the team reached out and picked up items from these piles. As they moved their torch light surfaces refracted and reflected the light sending spectrum of colours sometimes into the safe and sometimes into their eyes. With the items in their hands they could see grey stones, like gravel, but gravel with reflecting surfaces. Scintillating. Some of the stones were crystalline but others more of a conglomeration. As they looked more colours were apparent in the stones. At the bottom of the safe were three bricks of cash, £50 notes wrapped in plastic. Beside them were six tin cans, looking most out-of-place like tins of beans in a pantry.

"Leave the cash, don't move that. Bring all the stones and the cans, Lock open a bag wide will you?" and with that the Consultant pulled the top drawer from the safe. The others spread out to let him past and then Safe and Glazier formed a pair and the company set to gently pouring the contents of the shelves into holdalls. They didn't know that they were undoing hours of work spent grading and valuing the stone, they just got to the task in-hand of getting the stones into bags so that they could carry them off. The Consultant then lifted one of the bags down from a desk feeling the weight of it. He knew he should be pleased, but already he was thinking. "How am I ever going to shift all these uncut diamonds."

21

The egress had been planned and practiced and that plan swung into play. Safe closed up and wiped down. Everyone still had gloves on but, nevertheless, everything that they touched was wiped by all the team as they left. Nothing remained to show that they had been there. Amateurs and addicts trash the places they rob (and sometimes the Consultant would do that to cover tracks) but the longer that their presence went undetected this time, the better. It was only minutes from the safe being opened until they formed up to exit and this was a critical point. They had stolen goods on them know, this was the 'caught red handed time' so they had to be prepared and move swiftly. For all they knew the opening of the safe, or the moving of the tantalising cash could have started a silent alarm. Kid was radioed as they prepared. It was expected that she would be asleep and woken. Her response was welcome. Just as they were thinking of radioing again a sleepy voice came back, "reading you lima charlie."

The Consultant smiled, the kid had been paying attention and had responded that they had been heard loud and clear. "OK, this is the count of five." That was the signal from the Consultant that they were going to leave in five seconds and they had the expectation that the alarm would sound again. For the second time that night precise actions were taken. Kid was practiced in the count and went through her steps. She took the keys, leaving the passenger side door open, opened the rear doors, opened the boot and boot cover and finally opened the driver's door and on the count of five put the key into the ignition. The alarm sounded as the fire door was swung open. Could the alarm be louder now? Had the passage of time and the silence of the night made the alarm grow in volume? Its wail flooded the suburb and washed back as an echo off the houses and buildings nearby. They must be quick. Lock had all the tools and the VCR and slung that bag deep into the boot. Glazier brought one holdall and pushed that into the boot and then he and Lock slid out the original toolbox that had come from the office. It was heavy and made an awful noise (but less than the wail of the alarm) when set onto its casters on the loading bay floor as the tools and other contents fell back into place. Safe and the Consultant had emerged with the fake toolbox and placed it into the boot where its doppelganger had just been. Kid climbed into the car and slid across the back seat. The Consultant didn't return to the building he stood by the fire door as Glazier, Lock and Safe emerged with the last of the bags. As Safe passed by the fire door was closed to silence the alarm. The ringing in their ears remained for a confusing moment. The crew took their seats as the Consultant closed the boot and ran to the driver's seat. If they were being sucked into an elaborate trap this is when it would be sprung. This was the time as they were all in the same place with all their tools and the loot. It couldn't be more red-handed than the red lead painters in a shipyard.

As the doors closed (no slamming) the car was started and they departed, promptly, but without drama. Screaming wheels is for the movies and not the suburbs of Cheltenham. It was only as the Consultant swung onto the road that he switched on the car's lights. He was all eyes as they rolled along. The more distance they started to cover the more he relaxed and started to breathe. Everyone was on the alert scanning the windows for any evidence of a trap being sprung. The route he took had several dependencies but consisted of short sections with turnings to make it difficult to follow and then a long slow drive down Leckhampton Road where it was much easier to check for anything or anyone following. The trip 'home' took on a familiar stillness, people were tired, they started to relax and then there were several short stops where people jumped out. Each disrobed from their PPE and gloves leaving those in the car. Each stop was close to an alleyway and Safe, Lock and Glazier headed down their alley and off to their transport and house. The last stop was a drive to the kid's house and she was dropped off. Her dad had evidently stayed up and came swiftly out, the Consultant's initial thought was that was to greet the child and make sure they were OK, but the kid was just pushed towards the house and without ceremony the question was asked "what have we got, is it money?"

"Not ready money, no. Nothing that we can split quickly. You know the drill. The kid goes to school as normal and you come to see me at twelve. I will see you then." It was said with finality, but it seemed to take a long time for the kid's father to close the car door, he seemed unwilling to let it go. But it would seem that he resolved that he would pick this up tomorrow and he watched the taillights disappear around the corner.

A long night continued for the Consultant. He had been trusted to hold everything that they had stolen and he also had all the other 'going equipped to steal' items. This was part of the plan. The others left him holding the baby and it was his primary task to now destroy as much evidence, as quickly as possible, as he could.

The Consultant had a great cover business for his profession, he was a scrap dealer. Not the pile of junk outside your house type, or a stack of cars leaking fluids into your garden type. Gold was his metal of choice but he liked metallurgy and could render down many metals into ingots. This work involved shredding and heat and he deployed both to obliterate links to that night's activities. He could throw away the Range Rover, but he had other plans for that and on arriving home he rang a number and asked for "a collection." He was told "it would be thirty minutes."

He fired up his furnace and emptied the car. The swag was put to one side and the combustibles went into the top of the furnace and metals (within the tool kit) and the toolbox were loaded into the shredder. Imagine a paper shredder on steroids. Into the shielded top you could put nigh-on anything and following a cacophony of noise that would make you grimace, inch long shreds fell from the base. It was a big machine, he had a hoist, rolling on a ceiling beam to get large items into the thing and he used that to drop the toolbox into the maw. The output still had paint and could, theoretically, be put back together as an evidence jigsaw, but it was pushed into a bucket, that also attached to the hoist and the debris was moved into the furnace.

Whilst this was ongoing a light flashed to show that the driveway was being used and the Consultant went out to meet someone who had come for the car. A motorbike approached and the pillion stepped off. The Consultant pointed to the Range Rover and the guy jumped in and drove off. This was a scheme that he had put together some years previously and, for those in-the-know, you could ask for a collection and your car would disappear. You get 10% of its market value and whilst that is a small return it's 10% more than pushing it off a cliff or burning it out. The beauty is that the destinations change but hold the same requirements; they are off grid in that the car arriving is not recorded or even noted as being close to the collection point and they are either quickly stripped or shipped abroad in an unidentifiable state. Essentially the

Range Rover and any forensic evidence had just vanished.

Dawn was still some hours away as the Consultant donned an overall and burned the last of the clothing and finished the pour. Mild steel and aluminium in the main that would need much further work, but he had got to a point where the furnace could be turned off and a relative quiet settled into his barn as metal pinked and ticked in their contractions. The barn had a door facing away from the house and he took that door, his dog and a bag of the diamonds. The autumnal cold struck him as he left the warmth of the barn and this quickened his step. It was only a short walk to the woodlands that bounded that side of his property and it was a straight path that he took at least once daily so it was with practiced steps that he entered the copse and took a well-worn path that met with another shared with other dog walkers. His dog was instantly distracted by scents but kept up with his master. The pair then struck off from that path under a beech, crunching through the mast husks. This led down to a depression bounded by high trees. Here he waited and listened. He could have been watched, he could have been followed, but to see him now that he had descended here, you would need to be very close. In the summer he could have expected to hear something, but in the cold of autumn, nothing stirred. He used a red torch to retain his night vision and searched the ground, it still took some finding with the season's leaf fall but he found the edge of a trapdoor and used that to find a large metallic flap, below which there was a keypad. He punched numbers and heard a whir and lifted the door to find a deep cupboard. The bag was deposited and the door closed. The door had camouflage fixed onto it, so all that was then needed was for the disturbed leaves to be replaced before he turned off his light and stood up. He listened hard, slowly revolving and then headed back to make another trip…there were a lot of diamonds.

Ultimately the task was complete. Evidence of the theft was off his property (but cached securely) and all other evidence destroyed. If he had the time and less adrenalin he may have slept soundly. As it was he showered, ate breakfast and tried to sleep on the sofa in the kitchen. He could only allow himself ninety minutes sleep and he checked the time as the alarm went off and got into a coffee as Safe and Lock arrived together. Whilst the physical evidence was gone, the team needed to also be disbanded, they needed to head in different directions.

22

"You look like shit."

"I didn't get my beauty sleep. I have a pot of coffee on. So everything is OK?" Both Lock and Safe nodded and grunted in the affirmative and took a seat. It was a good room. A typical Cotswold kitchen, expensive fitted kitchen and integrated appliances around flagstone floors and stone walls, AGA, large dining table, dog and lounging area looking through French doors into an enclosed garden. Much less formal than the room across the hallway, but this was a more relaxed meeting. On the table was a cafeteria, buns, some synthetic gloves, cut and uncut diamonds and one of the strange tin cans. They ate and drank and looked over the sample items. It was noted that the can sounded like a maraca when it was shaken and Lock was allowed to do the honours and took a tin opener from the kitchen drawer and after some encouragement and assurance he took the lid off. The expectation was akin to unwrapping a surprise present and all three of them converged to see what was revealed as the lid was removed. Not much was the initial impression, the can did look like it contained an assortment of pebbles and it was only when it was gently emptied onto the draining board that they spotted uncut diamonds within the contents. With their eye-in on what they should be looking for they started to prod the pile of stones and separate the contents and then gained an appreciation for what they had. A tin of assorted pebbles and uncut diamonds. They decided it was distinctly odd and then scooped the content back into the tin, washed the sandy debris remaining into the sink and resumed the coffee and buns. The Consultant spoke mid bun.

"I will be honest with you both, I am at a loss at how I am going to move this."

"Do you have an idea of how much this is all worth?" asked Safe.

"Not really" the Consultant reached out to prod the small pile of items on the table. A cut diamond described a circle as it rolled on the table. I am assuming that these are all diamonds by-the-way and I think you would need to be an expert to know their value. It's based on cut, carats, colour and there is something else."

"Clarity" said Lock examining one of the larger cut items.

"Yep, that as well, so I don't know if it is thousands or multiple thousands that are on the table. And we have bags of the stuff and I've not opened all the pouches and that was the first of the tins." The Consultant put his head in his hands then pulled himself together a bit and moved instead to run his fingers through his hair as he then sat upright in his chair and took a swig of coffee "but this is a good problem to have. We always thought there was something of value and we were right. As for the uncut diamonds, they would be even more difficult to value. But it looks like that is what this company was doing. I will have to look into it but they have amassed a lot of diamonds, importing them parcel-post to avoid someone looking into their dealings."

Safe was also prodding the cut items and watching the

stones catch the lights as they moved, seemingly mesmerised. "Well. As the lucky one from this group who has actually bought a diamond ring for the wife, that was a darn sight smaller than these and that cost me an arm and a leg. So just what's on the table must be worth thousands. We did well!" But then there was a 'but'. One of those that is drawn out to emphasise that it was a big but. "But you *can* shift it?"

"I'm going to have to research it and make a plan. You know the score Safe, if it were cash or something I could easily move then I would be transferring cash into your accounts now and we would be dividing stuff up. As it is I would love you to take one of the bags with you, you would save me a headache, but what's each bag worth? What's the split? This is *big*. There is a fortune for all of us here" he leaned back and opened his arms expansively. The Consultant tried to sound triumphant but Safe looked despondent as he looked up to the ceiling, he could see the looming problem.

"But it's not real. You got me into this as one, big, last, score. I went in blind and despite all the risks we are still blind…we have a pile of rock and no cash and I know you think you can work miracles but how are you going to change this into folding money? And do it without us all going to nick." Safe had pointed and waved his hands as that was said. He wasn't happy. Of all those in the team he had the experience and knew that fencing stolen goods wasn't easy, you lost value with each transaction, sometimes only getting back a fraction of what you stole was actually worth. Plus, with each move you exposed yourself and all those around you to questions.

The Consultant recognised the situation for what it was and knew that Safe would calm down. Lock was new to this and would be led by Safe. The clock ticked the Consultant did not offer excuses or half-baked plans, he just let Safe get used to the change in circumstances. Safe would eventually accept where they were and come to his own plan.

"Well. We had better get the hell out of dodge" he said with resignation.

"Your wife is at your place in Portugal?"

"Yep, went a week ago."

"OK. I have arranged passage exactly as before. For Lock's benefit, the car that brought you here will take you to Hamble on the South Coast, there's a pub there and you will be met and sailed to France in a small yacht; not quick, but it avoids passport control and you can learn how to sail if you're interested. There will be plenty of traffic sailing the channel, even at this time of the year. If anyone asks you are doing a Competent Crew course. Safe, it's the same skipper and boat as before. Lock, it's down to you what you do then. Clearly Safe will head South."

"It's OK, Safe has already suggested I go to his place and take in the sun." The two of them exchanged a smile and Safe continued as he picked one of the more impressive cut diamonds and placed it into the palm of his hand.

"Yep, I could see this coming a mile off. I can see you have a job on your hands with this, I am not sure if we will ever see the proceeds of it" he shook his head sadly and placed the diamond back onto the table as if he was saying goodbye to it. "I will introduce the lad to the wife and continue his bad education."

"OK I will leave it to the two of you to make your way South. If you need help then ask, but it won't be quick as I'm not a miracle worker." There was a sniff at that gentle jibe.

"Here's an advance. There's also details of bank accounts in there and I will transfer cash when I can." A drawer was opened and two envelopes slid across the table. "Twenty grand. It's all I had at hand to spare now and you do have your own passports?" They nodded assent and patted pockets.

"And how long are we going to live on twenty grand?" Safe said without malice.

The Consultant started to stand to indicate that the meeting was coming to an end and said "that's my problem to solve but I will look to do it quickly and get cash wired into those accounts as and when." He realised that he had finished on a despondent note so reached out to shake hands with them both and held onto Safe's hand. "You were right in what you said, it's not going to be easy to change this into cash and I won't take risks to do it. But I'd like to think that I will be sending you each a substantial amount."

Safe nodded in resignation and then extracted his hand and took off his gloves and dropped them into the fireplace where they shrivelled to nothing in seconds. Like their hopes for a quick fortune from this job. They made vague promises to see each other on the beach when all was settled and with that they were waved off to get out of the country as quickly and as quietly as possible. Safe stood at the door of the car and thought that he had absolutely nothing to show for the risks that he had taken. At least he had not been nicked but perhaps he wouldn't be able to return to Cheltenham ever. The Consultant said 'he needed time', but Safe wasn't confident that this was doable, even by the Consultant. As he worked to sell the diamonds more risks would be taken, but it would be the Consultant who was holding the baby and would be taking the risks. It was out of his hands now. So he raised his hand as a salute and got into the car. It was for The Consultant to pull this out of the fire.

23

Glazier was the next to arrive, brought by car as per the others and the original plan was to send him abroad on a yachting trip too. He would travel separately and under a false passport (in case he was asked to show one by the harbourmaster on arrival in a small French port). His situation was slightly different, his potential involvement would be apparent with his disappearance. He would become the prime suspect. The Consultant sat him down with a coffee after waving the car away. They sat with a corner of the table between themselves, so kind of side-on, less awkward and less confrontational as this was bad news.

"Let's start with the good news. We have scored big here, there is a fortune in diamonds in those bags. I don't know how much, but it's enough to keep a family business in comfortable wealth. More good news is that it's pretty untraceable. But the bad news is that I don't know where to sell it, or who would buy it. Now, I have moved diamonds before, but in all my years of moving dodgy stuff I have moved less diamonds than are in your hand and there are more on the table and we have bags of uncut diamonds. My hope was that we would split the take today and head off into the sunset with nothing to tie us to the job. But I will need to come up with a plan on how I turn this…" and with that there was a wave in the general direction of the diamonds… "into cash. With Lock and Safe I can send them off and they will not be missed or noticed, they won't be suspects or linked to this, but you will be missed. If you stay at your place you will have the finger pointed at you soon as being potentially involved. So you need to go to ground. I would send you out of the country, but I would rather do that when I know we will actually get some money out of this."

Glazier caught the doubt in his voice, there was disbelief that this could all come to naught. "But surely we will get money for this?"

75

"At the moment it's like the Mona Lisa, how do you sell it without whoever you approach going 'isn't that's the missing Mona Lisa?' I have done jobs where it's easier to bury the loot than move it; especially if selling it will get me caught."

"Hang on. Rewind that a bit" Glazier now sat forward, his disbelief was moving to understanding and he switched from the seemingly mild-mannered bod into perhaps the person that had gone into young offenders. The Consultant remained impassive but inwardly surprised "you are telling me that I have shat my life over and my job over and I could end up with *nothing*?"

"What I am telling you is that it's going to take longer to realise cash from bags of uncut diamonds, I know what you have risked for this. You *will be* a rich man. It's there in front of you, but I need time to convert it. And in that time you should go to ground here. When we have the cash then we are off to the beach." The Consultant had nearly convinced himself with that exposition. Glazier slowly deflated and sank back into his seat, the colour drained from his face as his furrowed brow unknitted itself.

"Nothing to do but wait then."

"Well, there's always something to do, the news will start to break soon so it would be good if you can monitor what the news and police are saying. And you can also look into the diamond business. We need to find out what the bean tins are about. I will get you a laptop and there's a radio tuned to the police band in the lounge. Kid's dad is coming to visit and I don't need you two to meet. First thing though, give me a hand to move these." He started to pick up the items on the kitchen table and Glazier helped to place them in a room off the kitchen. It was a cross between a panic room and strong room. An elaborate system protected the data within it. There was a rack of PCs, lots of computer screens, locked drawers and a good sized safe under a desk. As he went in Glazier noted the thickness of the door and did a double take as he went back into the kitchen of how normal the exterior of the door looked; in keeping with the other doors off the kitchen. The door closed with a clunk.

Glazier got settled listening into the police and with a laptop. The Consultant was jealous of how comfortable he looked in the lounge doing his research. He wanted to sleep, his head was now pounding and he took pain killers and coffee and tried to get some time to think. He hadn't had much time that day to stop. It was vital to clear decks before the police came (and they would) and that had been largely achieved promptly. Car gone, physical evidence degraded and destroyed, the team dispersed or close by. Only the Kid was unaccounted for, but he had a good feeling about the kid. He gave up trying to think about how to move the diamonds, that would only make his head hurt more. He decided to just rest a while, but that plan failed as he was alerted to someone coming down the drive.

The kid's father was early and the speed he came down the driveway showed some intent. Glazier was warned that they had a guest and to keep clear and the Consultant went outside to meet their visitor. This was cordial enough and neither wanted to start a discussion outside and they moved into the porch and went through the search and scan protocol. He had brought his phone. Displeasure was shown by the Consultant and a warning for next time to be more careful. The frisk gave a good chance to size him up. He was underweight but had clearly been fitter and built in the past, his manual labour still showed in his musculature and he had inches over the Consultant. His hands were clearly those of a mechanic so difficult so see if he had spent time punching bags, or people when younger. All in all, the Consultant thought it best to avoid fisticuffs. Even if they both seemed grumpy enough to try it today.

They were moving to sit in the kitchen, as with the others and the Consultant was about to gently explain the situation but was beaten to it by some accusations.

"I want to know what's going on, I'm getting a feeling that you're cutting me out." An accusatory finger was jabbed. The Consultant was keen to sit down and laid his hands flat on the table ahead of himself.

"No. I am not going to cut anyone due a share out of their share. It's not the way I work."

"Good, so where is my share?"

"Your *kid's* share and all the rest of the team are going to have to wait for me to move the goods and get you cash that you can use."

"So how much am I getting and when?" The accusatory finger was jabbed at the table to emphasise 'when'.

"I don't know how much or when. We are in a complicated situation."

"Why's it complicated?" He shook his head and winced in fake confusion. "You all went out last night and robbed somewhere and I want my slice, you seem to be busy telling me nothing. What did you steal?"

The volume was being raised here and the Consultant decided to count to ten before his next statement as it was going to be provocative. He only got to five as he was losing patience himself but worked to keep his heartbeat, breathing and demeanour calm.

"I am not going to tell you. You do not need to know. You have separation from what we did last night and that's the way it's going to stay. You are asking questions that I don't have the answers to yet. You are also asking questions that I don't want to answer. What I can tell you is that your kid will get their fair share when I am able to share it. And I will be frank, all you need to do is carry on with your life and send your kid to school and soon you will get access to a new bank account that you didn't even know you had."

"But when? You must have *some* idea?"

"I need to come up with a plan. That will take a while and then I will be able to consider how long it will take to deliver that plan."

The kid's dad did take a seat but pulled a sour face and leaned back whilst crossing his arms. "So you're telling me to piss off, be quiet, leave you to make your plans and all will be fine." He began to lean forward again and lowered his voice and bared his teeth as he emphasised the next statement. "You think I'm soft in the head" the accusatory finger was jabbed again "you posh Cheltenham twats see dirt under my nails and think I've dirt between my ears. You have kept me in the dark but I know enough." He spread his arms around and opened his eyes wide "I'm in your house, I know it was you who did *something* so I'm not going to be cut out and I am not going to wait around so that you can piss off to your Swiss chalet leaving me looking like I've not got a partner when *Careless Whisper* comes on at the disco." There was a count to ten now. The Consultant took his hands from the table and leaned in, he didn't know if he sounded menacing, but he tried.

"First up. I'm not a *Cheltenham* twat. I'm from Gloucester. You know what the situation is. I do know that *you* know who I am and where I live. However, I don't think you really know *who* I am. You seem to have implied that you would tell someone what you know and I'm telling you to never make such a statement again. I live by a few rules and one of them is *never* to rat. And if I thought that you would talk to the police then it would sour our relationship." He leaned back at this point "as it stands you do need to wait. I can assure you, I don't want to wait long either. I don't think that there is more I can do for you now. Just act naturally and keep your kid in school."

Neither party was happy. There was a threat and

counter threat and long stare to finish. The kid's dad got up and left saying nothing more and leaving doors open as he went.

The Consultant thought he would be back soon. That was the loosest of loose ends. He had made a mistake there. He rang his solicitor and invited him round for a late lunch and went to sleep.

24

DCI Grace and DC Harper had removed the dividers from their desks many moons ago and arranged things so that they faced one another over keyboards, PCs, screens, staplers, pens, cacti, coasters, mugs and other office detritus that gathers outside of the 'clean desk' policy. The effort to remove barriers had been hampered by needing the PC screen at eye-level (as per the computer-based training on posture etc) and so leaning or doing a meerkat impression was needed to get eye contact. Presently both were head-down and busy in the morning sweet spot of energy working on the same task for an upcoming court appearance. His phone rang and Harper jabbed the speaker button on his desk phone without really looking up and announced himself without appellation or enthusiasm as 'Harper'.

"Sir, there's been a burglary…"

"We don't do burglaries" responded both Grace and Harper in a simultaneous response that they had practiced several times before when talking to their operations desk and they kept on working as before without changing their demeanour.

"The robbery squad are all out and busy and so we were not sure what to do with it so I was told to pass it to you."

"Haven't we sent a PC to attend?"

"Yep, we have done that PC Ravi is on his way." Ravi was a longstanding PC based in the Leckhampton office and useful for such little local issues, but he wasn't quick (in a few ways) and would be cycling to the crime scene. The days of a car park full of high-powered patrol cars was long gone.

"And no one was injured, because you know this office deals with assaults and homicides?"

"No-one was injured."

At this point Harper was a little agitated and his train of thought had jumped the tracks and was rolling down an embankment. He picked up the phone handset to cut off the speaker.

"So, no one is injured, a PC is on the way and you know that we don't do robberies; so *please* tell me why are you ringing this desk?" There was a dialogue that Grace could no longer hear (and that suited her) so she was a little taken aback as Harper, still on the phone, rose to his feet and reached behind himself for his jacket and started the elaborate, flailing dance, of trying to put on a jacket using only one arm. "OK, say the address again. We will be there in about ten minutes."

Grace leaned back and restated "we don't do burglaries" but Harper ushered her to her feet and started for the door himself.

"But this one sounds like a good one boss. It could be that someone is exaggerating or has put a colon in the wrong place but the 999 caller said there was five million pounds that was stolen." Grace checked herself and looked a little non plussed and confused. Harper passed her coat and again ushered her to the door "and so this could be the biggest robbery in the southwest...well ever! So I think we had better have a look as leaving it to PC Ravi on his Raleigh Chopper could bite us both on the arse."

They headed out still discussing 'we don't do robberies' (or they hadn't for a while since covering themselves in glory in a prior case and moving upwards) but it was close by and Harper was happy to have a look at a robbery, it was his old stomping ground as a PC and he liked to see if he could spot any peculiarities in the MO and link them to anyone he knew. He was good at that. It had lifted him from the norm of a PC into CID. That took him some years but now he made a great partnership with Grace as he had the years of experience and knowledge and she had the modern criminology theory and a much quicker mind. Her hard work had made her clever and his hard work had made him wise.

As they travelled down the Lansdown Road and headed to Leckhampton they discussed the larger robberies in Gloucestershire and it was clear that in recent years there were many more street thefts and house burglaries than from a business, even banks and nothing near this size. Harper didn't know the business they were going to, so it flew under the radar for both of them and that was a small surprise that a business with such cash around wasn't one that the police knew about; but they agreed that they were not omnipotent.

They pulled up, strategically blocking the entrance and stood on the pavement looking at the property. It was a small, self-contained and innocuous unit on a trading estate. No flags or hoardings, all rather subdued. There was a cycle leaned against the wall and PC Ravi walked towards them. Harper led.

"Hi Ravi. What's going on?"

"Well…" he looked into his notebook "guard opened up at 8.30 and didn't notice anything amiss and got on with having a cuppa and the office manager came in just after nine and it was only when he opened the safe at around 10 that he realised that its contents were gone…and the contents were £5million of diamonds. So I have come over and given a crime reference and suppose you want to get SOCO to have a look. But why are you two here anyway, no-one has died?"

"You could be first on the list" said Harper only half-jokingly "£5million of diamonds! Are we sure on that as if

83

it's that big then yes, we will have SOCO, the chief constable and Kate Aide here in no-time. This is big Ravi. Get everyone out of the building, tape off the whole street and list everyone's comings and goings through a cordon that you will set up here. It's a major crime scene until we say that it isn't. We will get more bodies to assist. Is that the office manager coming over?"

It was. And Ravi got busy with tape and Harper introduced Grace who picked things up as they ushered the manager outside of the cordon being setup across the car park gates.

He was tall, well built, worked out, well-manicured, well-dressed, in an office casual way and even smelt good. He oozed wealth and Grace liked him instantly and she checked that he did have a wedding band. Harper took an instant dislike to the well coiffured, tanned and good-looking guy.

"So you are?"

"I am the managing director James De Jong, this is my family's business. We have been diamond dealers for some generations and this is a bit of a shock to the system, it's all gone, everything." He did look shocked.

"And you are sure on the valuation, are we talking about a large number of diamonds?"

"It's not the amount, it's the quality. One diamond could have a value in excess of that sum; but our diamonds are not all of high value, we buy uncut diamonds and have them worked to increase their value. Some will make valuable gemstones and others not-so, relatively speaking. The monetary value is therefore difficult to land on, but I am sure that £5million would be our loss. Unless you can find them?"

"That's our job Mr De Jong. Can I say that we..." at this she gestured to Harper and herself but, through implication meant the police... "didn't know that such valuables were here. When was the last time you saw them?"

"Well, we don't trade with the public, it's very much the wholesale market and we are well known in the right circles, but that is the London and Netherlands and I locked up Thursday and all was normal then."

Harper offered "so not many people know what you do here. How many staff have you got?" Straight to the inside job theory thought Grace.

"Only five who deal with the diamonds, but they are all family. We have cleaners, IT and security, but we try to ensure that what we do isn't obvious to those outside the family. And we would like to keep it that way. The less this gets out the better, we have been in this office for many years, we wouldn't want to move if we can help it."

"Well, we will need names for everyone on the payroll and this will get out. This may be amounts that you are used to, but this is a large robbery for Cheltenham police. It is going to make news. We will get the scene of crimes team here now and let them get through the building first and record what evidence they can. From the timings of this it seems they left very little trace. It took some time for you to notice the theft?"

"Well, yes, it was only when I opened the safe that I noticed anything was wrong."

"I think the best thing to do is to list those with access to the safe as a start-point."

"But it's only my family that know the combination?" Grace and Harper exchanged a look and Harper stated the obvious.

"Well, that would point to one of them opening the safe. List their names and addresses and we will see where they were overnight."

"OK. I will let them know of the theft and we will have to get together anyway" you could see his mind planning this out "we will need to meet as a board, notify the insurers and get the news out; as we should warn the other dealers to be on the look-out for someone trying to sell our diamonds. OK, I will give you a list of their names and get everyone together this afternoon so you can talk to them. I do understand that you will want to look at those who work here first so the sooner you check that off the better."

Grace and Harper also had to get balls in motion and placed Mr De Jong in their car to make his calls and they made their calls to get more personnel on the ground. She suggested that if the press were going to attend, one PC on a bike wasn't a good look. The mention of press and political decisions (with a small p) had more bodies in hi-vis arrive with the SOCO team. They were pleased that Grace and Harper had closed things off. The only people in that morning was Ravi, the office manager and the guard. They set to work starting on any tyre tracks or footprints in the car park. A long shot, but Grace knew that any scrap of evidence could be useful here as, if this was an inside job, then familiar DNA would be all over the property. If they found no foreign fingerprints, hair, tracks or *anything* then it would add weight to the inside job theory. Whilst they waited for SOCO to get into the property they talked to the security guard. He was smartly dressed in dark suit and tie, all good quality, clean and not worn. He was late fifties perhaps, a little overweight but not unhealthily so. He did have a military air as he marched over to them after being beckoned. He instinctively stood to attention as Harper kicked off.

"So, you are security here?"

"It's a grand title really, I am more of a receptionist most of the time. I unlock, lock up, look after the CCTV tapes and sweep up. It's a great job, I have been here nine years in May, it pays well, is inside work and is no trouble. Their security is good. I have keys" and with that he lifted a ring with a few keys attached "but they only get me into a few doors. You may not believe this but I have only been into a few rooms of the building and I don't know what they have inside there. If I am lucky with doors being open then I can see their safe, when I go to Mr De Jong's office for example. But that suits me, if I am security then the less people who knows what's inside the better so I am not nosy."

"Who comes and goes, who does know what goes on in there?"

"Gardener, window cleaner, couriers, IT guy, finance bod now and again but mainly it's the family. Old man De Jong employed me, I was ex-military…" (Harper wondered how long it would be before he mentioned that and wasn't surprised that he started reciting his service career before being brought back on track)… "so it was he and his late brother for a bit and then the sons and their wives came in. I saw them grow up and now they manage the place." He seemed to have run out of steam. Harper wanted to inject some steam.

"Where's the friction, which of the sons wants their inheritance early?" The security guy looked a bit taken aback but thought on the question, scratching his neck and pulling a grimace. Grace took her turn in applying the pressure.

"Look, I am sure you are a good guy, but the way this goes with this type of job is we look at the family first and then at the security guard quickly after. Fingers will be pointed to you. You should get in their first." They both liked the direct route.

"It's nothing to do with me, I'm not going to crap on my own doorstep. This is a great job and retirement is round the corner for me. So look at the family if you like, but they have all been great to me. Go looking for skeletons in closets and all that but they look a tight and normal family, albeit with loads of cash."

"So business is good?"

"So I am told. I don't see the books but I do see a rise every April, my Christmas bonus, clothes allowance and a hamper. So as I said, it's a great job, lovely family and I've not taken more than a stapler in all these years." Harper was going to crawl over this guy's past, but he seemed to be the loyal retainer at the moment. He looked at Grace, who had no objections to his changing tack.

"Talk us through this morning, step by step and in detail please."

"8.30 is my start time so was here 8.25 and my way in is via the Rolladoor. There's a key for up and down. The alarm beeped as normal and I put the code in to turn it off. Next thing I did was to put the lights on in the loading bay and go to my office. The CCTV tape had ejected as it had reached the end and that's not unusual so I put the old one on the shelf, dated the new one as today and put that in the recorder. I started my PC and whilst it was booting put the kettle on. I've a key to get from the loading bay to the kitchen, toilet and a meeting room. I don't have a key for the gate, the other doors and clearly not the safe. I took the tea back to my office. By the way, I call it an office, but it's just a room with windows so that I can see who comes and goes. I checked diaries for any callers or maintenance to arrange and expected an easy day. There wasn't a board meeting or anything. James, that's Mr De Jong the eldest son, arrived just after nine and we had a chat about the weather and football, we got a coffee then he went through the gate to his office and I was planning to wash his car. About ten he came out looking pale and said there had been a robbery, the safe was empty, he had rung the police and asked if I had seen anything to which I said that I hadn't. I said we could look at the CCTV but he had been told not to touch anything so we waited in the loading bay. Then your lad cycled up. That wasn't the response we were expecting. Don't you have panda cars now?" Silence fell and that was clearly the end of the narration.

Grace smiled the sweetest of smiles "we do have cars, but also a tight budget. But we are here now in numbers and we will be spending large efforts on finding out who did this. Your background and associations will be looked at closely. Statistically speaking, you are very much in the frame."

The security guard looked worried and looked between Harper and Grace and only saw stern faces "do I need a solicitor or something?"

"Do you plan on writing a will or buying a house?" offered Harper and received a quizzical look in response "as that's what law abiding people use solicitors for. You just need to be clear with us now if there is anything else that you want to say. Are you the disgruntled employee, have you been approached by bad men offering large sums, seen anything suspicious, had threats made, anything like that, stuff that happens to people in your role that make them stray from the path" as he said that Harper stepped slightly forward, set himself square in-front of the security guard and leaned forward, not intimidating in itself but certainly a pointed language to emphasise that 'now was the time'. The security guard wasn't fazed or annoyed by the challenge, his eyes flicked as he was thinking but was then clear.

"I have nothing to help you. The only odd thing about this job is that I don't know what they all do here; but this is Cheltenham, there are loads of 'civil servants' and IT people who won't tell you where they work or what they do. And I am used to that secrecy. If I don't know what's here then why would anyone else. You guys know, banks get robbed as people know they have cash in them. Here, no-one knows."

"Or knew. I think the secret is out now" stated Grace, who didn't like being referred to as 'guys' but did agree with the points made that she knew plenty about bank robberies and that the largest employer in Cheltenham was the Government Communications Head Quarters where most of their employees evaded saying where they worked. They placed him into another car and would have his statement later and turned to see progress. The scenes of crime were into the building now and Grace and Harper could start their approach with clearance from the SOCO lead.

"Any tracks?"

"It's a car park so lots. Really faint though. The most recent are from that Merc" he jabbed over his shoulder with his pen "and most of the tracks are very similar to it, new tyres, clear treads. Perhaps the company cars are Mercs. But there is a different set by that fire door, large SUV from the tyre size and track width and reversed in. I would say they are recent as we can make them out, but really faint, I'd be sticking my neck out to get a pattern or manufacturer, it's really just marks in dust."

They went in via the loading bay Rolladoors and surveyed the scene. James' car was there, the glass office and little else of note. Bucket and hose made ready for car cleaning, although it wasn't that dirty. Just something for a bored security guard to do. If he was involved he was being as cool as an Icelandic cucumber. They chatted and called back the security guard and he told them how to lower and raise the Rolladoor and it made the predictable clamour of metal-on-metal screeches as the large door slowly rolled itself. So that confirmed their thoughts and the importance of the tracks by the fire door. SOCO were looking closely at the door and the tracks within the dust around it. They asked the security guard about the toolbox.

"It was here when I started, I suspect it came with the building and it's fine. I use the tools from time to time, but the De Jong's expect me to call a plumber or electrician as needed. I don't do maintenance. Much of the maintenance is on contracts. The gas man, electrician, they all come regularly." He confirmed he had not moved it or been near it for some time. He agreed that the tracks were therefore relevant. Whilst relevant, not overly useful as all SOCO could say was that overshoes had been used. They could all look and guess at some shoe sizes and how many people were involved but the tracks were as faint, just marks in dust and then they disappeared into the carpeted floors. Grace and Harper walked the corridor and squeezed by the individuals brushing talcum and graphite powder onto the three doors. They stopped and looked over shoulders to see how the locks looked and they both saw the concentric rings of security. Less people had access to the sanctum and the physical security improved with each ring. They could only stand at the doorway of the final room and look toward the safe, ringed with bright lights and the crouching white clad forensic team. They were like a congregation looking towards an alter while priests bent in supplication. They even hushed their voices for some reason.

"That's a big one."

"Said the actress to the bishop. I'm getting a sinking feeling that SOCO aren't going to get much, despite them covering the place in powder." Grace agreed and continued.

"So we need to see more of the family, look at all the employees, especially the security guy and look at the books, if they are rolling in money why steal your own diamonds?" and before Harper could answer Grace said what was on his mind "unless it's for insurance and I didn't miss the insurers being mentioned already but that need for five million pounds should be clear from the accounts. As James De Jong has arranged a meeting of the family let's look at the whites of their eyes and ask for access to their books."

"Hate to sound despondent ma'am, but I do hope that we find a brother with a massive coke habit and huge debts shivering at this family meeting to make our lives easy. If it's by outsiders they look to have covered their tracks well."

25

The De Jongs met at James' house and their father was the last to arrive. He hugged and kissed the wives and children, hugged his boys, took the offered tea and took his seat at the head of the dining table and opened business as he opened his notebook.

"How are the books?" James' wife answered leaning forward to get a good view down the table.

"Everything is up to date and in order, I expect some forensic analysis and there may be questions on expenses and tax paid, but they should be expecting to find something so" and at this point she looked around those at the table "don't worry about taxation and expenses questions I don't go overboard on those, I am bending rules not breaking, but I am pushing boundaries and was creative. Just push all the accounts questions my way."

"And the real books are not in the office or at home?"

"No, they are in a safe deposit box now. I will put the auditors on notice that the police will call." Papa De Jong ticked off some items in his notepad and turned to James.

"Talk us through what you saw."

"It was all in place on Thursday, Mark..." at this point he nodded to his brother across the table... "and I locked everything away as normal. So I did a double take when I opened the safe this morning and it was all gone. The cash was left behind, but all the diamonds are gone and the tins. All the locks, alarms and doors were unmarked. No smash

92

and grab."

"They left the cash? Who else knew about the serial numbers record and the dye trace on those?"

"Well, all of us and the security consultant as he recommended it, but it was years ago that he suggested that."

"OK, so it looks like they knew what they were doing. To get in and out without leaving a trace and being cautious enough to leave the cash. It doesn't help us as the police are going to focus on us. Expect them to search your houses, phones, computers and look into your friends too. You all need to account for movements over the week. Don't be vague, get into your phones and be sure where you were and when and who you were with. What you watched on TV, when you went to bed. If you have to change a story then they will be like a dog with a bone. They are going to waste time looking at us so give them what they need so they move onto whoever did this. Now..." at this point he shuffled forward in his seat and checked his notes and ticked another item off... "we have the advantage over the police as we know it's not an inside job and it would be good to ensure we get all our diamonds back before the police do. Peter, get onto all the dealers and let them know to be on the lookout for anyone new, large amounts, anything unusual. Janice, talk to De Beers and tell them the bad news. Mathew, get the insurers going on this. If we need to start from scratch then we will need that capital and it is five million pounds?" Mathew nodded in confirmation. "So that's important. Everyone be clear on that. The police and insurer will ask numerous times how much was stolen and our sum insured is five million pounds so be definitive on that. It's not roughly that, or could be around, be precise, choose your words carefully. Our estimated loss is five million. It goes without saying that no-one talks to the press and try to avoid photographs.

We can bounce back from this if we keep things as quiet as possible. Right," there was more shuffling and a pregnant pause for effect "who do we think did it?" Papa De Jong raised his voice for those last words and scanned those around the table. No-one looked guilty, just perplexed. "All of you ring your couriers. Get them talking about their week, be very social at first and see if they are nervous. Every one of them needs to be accounted for. Then pass on the bad news and let them know that there will not be packages for a while but be positive and they will resume in due course. Remind them to keep their mouths shut about the packages. Warn them that they will get questioned by the police as they are all on payroll and the police will be talking to everyone. So they need to be expecting the police to question them and they shouldn't worry about that. But we need to know where they all were last night. Is there anybody we are nervous about?"

"Well Sam has the best access" offered James and this was true as Sam was the security guard.

"Well, this is where the police earn the tax we do pay. They can work out how the robbers got in and can see if Sam has suddenly turned to crime. He has been with us since the start, it would be odd to now decided to rob us. I'd be very surprised if he is involved especially as he is at work today. We are looking for who is missing. The window cleaner is the newest recruit. Start with him" and he nodded at Peter at that point and put a circle around Glazier's name on the notebook. "The police are due in half an hour anything else? The group shook their heads and broke up and started dialling numbers.

26

Grace and Harper were met at the door by James and introduced to papa De Jong and led into the kitchen. The house had been a farmhouse on the escarpment side of Cheltenham. No longer part of a farm, it was part of a nice sizeable garden and set well back along a pleasant drive. Harper particularly admired the way the floorboards and flagstones in the hallway flowed into a kitchen that then flowed into a dining room, but his gaze came up from the floor to the wall of glazing that showed the expansive view across the vale of Gloucestershire towards the Forest of Dean and Pen y Fan in Wales. Harper was reminded of houses he had seen in glossy magazines and Grace was reminded of her aunty Valarie's house.

The dining table had become boardroom table and the family tidied up papers and got reorganised as Grace and Harper were shepherded to the head of the table, Papa moved to the other end to face them, moving Peter who ended up moving into the meat of the table. Grace took control and clicked through items with speed; thank you for the invite, it was good use of everyone's time, there was a need to eliminate people from the investigation and a need to gather information so this unorthodox meeting seemed to meet lots of requirements. She asked for a round table introduction of who was in attendance and their roles. James went first but added nothing new and was brief handing onto Peter's wife as being a better person to talk about roles.

"My role is company secretary, I look after the legal and corporate side of things. And when I say legal I mean filing annual reports, audits, procedural items regarding structure and not criminal law. The group has a simple structure; my father in law is chairman of DJD Group and we are the board of DJD ltd a subsidiary of Group and we have a managing director..." James was pointed to using a Montblanc pen with a diamond in its tip... "financial officer..." that was James' wife "head of acquisitions is my husband Mathew and Peter is head of sales. Peter's wife holds the title of manager of support services but all of us have titles that are easy to apply but we all flex what we do, unless it comes to the diamonds then that is with the men" and at this point papa De Jong explained what they do.

"We buy from De Beers as packages of uncut diamonds. They do keep the best for themselves but they sell most of what they mine and our job is to buy raw, ungraded diamonds and as the aphorism goes, find the diamond in the rough. Our task is to sort them and decide the stones to cut, polish and improve. We don't do that processing here but contract that out. We sell the smaller and less valuable stones. Our efforts are to find the real gems and maximise their value. We then sell the output into retailers in London, Antwerp and sometimes New York. My father set the business up in 1930. He wasn't planning to stop in England but was going to the USA from Holland, but he liked the weather here and stayed. As I grew up my father passed on what he knew about diamonds and I have done the same with my boys. As has been stated, Mathew buys stock, Peter sells them, but all of us work in the grading and inspection. Their wives provide all the support the business needs and are experts in their field, being solicitors and accountants" each was nodded to in turn as this was said "before they came into the business as wives." All very cosy thought Grace, keep your secrets close. She turned to James' wife.

"So, you are the accountant?" this was confirmed by the nod of the head and Harper thought it was charming that her diamond earrings caught the light as her head moved. "How's business?"

"Well that's quite a general question but the general answer is 'good'. Turnover and profits are strong, we trade as a limited company so we file annual results and elect to be audited. The results have been strong since company inception. No losses in the available accounts, healthy balance sheet. I will expect that one of your colleagues with an understanding of these matters will need confirmation and access to bank details and the board have agreed to expedite that access without need of a warrant. I think I know what you will need so I will put a package together and send it on. I worked in tax and audit with one of the Big Four so am used to assisting forensic accountants."

"Did you, by any chance, audit this firm before you married into it?" asked Grace trying her best to sound neutral as Grace thought James was lovely and he seemed to have married brains and beauty.

"Well yes. You could say I did my due diligence, but if you are looking for someone who wants more than they are due, we have been married five years and have two children and are very happy within the family firm and wouldn't steal from it." But someone did. Grace tried another suspect.

"So as company secretary you could provide listing of the employees?" Mathew's wife turned slightly in her seat but remained reclined without a care in the world.

"Yes I can print it for you to take but it would be better to email it as an Excel file so that you can filter as I have added our role based access controls as columns so you can see those who have access to the building, those who have keys for certain areas, who has access to the safe and if they know one, or both of the combinations. I have added another tab for contractors and what they do, their length of service and highlighted those that come on site and then where they have access to. You have been to the office and know that there's a meeting room by the kitchen and that is the main limit of access, but the electrician and our IT man could go to more areas if escorted. Peter, Mathew and James know both combinations. I know the left one and Jane the right, as there is cash within the safe so we could theoretically arrange to both be present to open it should our husbands not be available, although we have not had occasion to do that. And I expect you to ask; I met my husband at work. I was a solicitor looking at the potential to set up the group and plc arrangement and we hit it off. We have been married nearly ten years and also have two children. I second Jane's view that I like being part of the family firm and would not steal from my family and would go as far as to say we don't need to. I am sure you can see that we are not in need of money."

Grace thought *that was comprehensive* and slid her business card down the table so that the file could be emailed whilst saying "appearances can be very deceiving. People can hide their secrets from their loved ones comprehensively. You are aware that we will look into your circumstances fully and if there are secrets we will expect to find them. It is what we do and we are very good at it. Whilst you want me to think of you as business professionals I get the feeling that you have little real work to do here, but can see lots of money moving about, perhaps you all got a little bored and over a long lunch you decided to show your men who is really in charge? And we come to the 'manager of support services' that's a made-up job title if I have ever heard one, you have been very quiet through all of this."

Grace turned to face the eldest lady at the table but mid-forties at most, modest (in this group) diamond necklace and Chanel dress with the thought that *if she wears a Chanel dress on Friday afternoons what must a night out be like.* Without a breath and despite the purposeful goading to the ladies at the table there was an instant response.

"I lost my grander titles as my sisters-in-law joined the firm. I was the company secretary and accountant previously but was happy to hand those tasks to the real experts as the business expanded. But I still need the made-up job title to draw my outrageous remuneration and to have my seat on the board. You are very perceptive Miss Grace, we do not have much to do with the working of the company but our husbands do, we support them when we need but they do the hard work and that does afford us plenty of time for long, lavish, lunches. I do hope that you will join us when your perspicacity has led to the recovery of our diamonds. And to compliment the others, I have been married nearly twenty years have two children too and all our children are in rather expensive schools paid for through an educational trust set up by DJD Group and I would add that I am independently wealthy. I have no need to steal from my own family and do not wish to find enjoyment through planning a robbery. I have plenty of imagination to find diversions without wrongdoing. So I really do believe that the thieves you are looking for are not at this table and are not involved with anyone within this room."

That was said with some firmness but also with a friendly smile. It did leave Harper reeling from the use of *perspicacity* in conversation outside of a Dickens novel. Grace turned to Harper and gave a slow blink as a sign that it was his turn. They had decided she would push the females and he the males, which he duly did.

"This all seems like sweetness and light" he proclaimed with his hands aloft "everyone is happy, dripping in diamonds and loves working here. Stupid plod needs to look elsewhere. James you are the youngest of three, it's crap being the youngest, I know..." (this wasn't actually true Harper was an only child but wanted to get on common ground with James) "...hand-me-downs, being belittled it's well known that the youngest wants to better their brothers and you know both combinations to the safe and were the last one to see the diamonds."

"Most of us know both combinations" he returned affably "and I suspect you are pushing for a rise out of us, but we are a close and loving family who work well together."

99

"Middle for diddle, you are neither first nor last and have been quiet in here too. Have a chip on your shoulder for lacking the respect of the eldest or not getting the love that goes to the youngest?"

This did seem to get a reaction. There was some anger in the response from Mathew, who leaned forward and put his elbows on the table to allow some expression from the arms he spread wide and pointed at the table to emphasis his points.

"Officers, you are looking for division where it doesn't exist. This faux psychology isn't moving this forward. As pointed out to you repeatedly by all of us, we work well together in a joint endeavour, we are good at what we do and recognise that in each other. We travel, work and holiday together, as well as apart. We would not steal from one another. You are looking in the wrong place for your criminals."

Both Grace and Harper thought that might be stretching the truth but both could not see a shivering coke hound with huge debts within the room. If anyone needed money they could sell the jewellery or watches they were wearing. The key to this was elsewhere. Grace re-iterated their thanks for the meeting, said that statements would be needed, that contact would be made for access to the books and they said their goodbyes; without making a lunch date.

27

They pulled into a farm gate a short distance away and got onto phones. There were many things to organise and they wanted PC Harrison in their new incident room to start ticking the items off by allocating tasks to the growing team. Priority items were to get people onto the financial data the firm was providing. Then a bio on all the family with personal financials and a review of any social media.

This was to close-off the search for the secret smack head with a huge gambling debt. Also, the background on the security guard, the non-family staff members and information from the insurer, alarm provider and initial SOCO findings. All were needed for their kick-off meeting plus a review of the CCTV. When they got off their phones they both sat for a few quiet seconds that Grace disrupted.

"If this isn't an inside job where do we go, what's in your data banks on this Harps?"

"Let's use the assumption that if we are in the dark on what that business has been doing for years, if they have flown under the radar on what they have in there, it must be someone local. Someone who knows what they were about and knew it was worth robbing. And if we proceed from there then it's a sophisticated local gang. There were plenty of footprints, they used a big car and needed a safe expert, as again, let's assume they didn't have the combinations. So between two or four bodies, I will go for four as you might need muscle. So someone local who can put a team together with the relevant skills and who have discipline to leave little trace. That could point to someone you may have heard of called the Consultant."

"I have not heard of him for a while. Is he still around?"

"Yep, I think so, still pulling strings and getting things done, but we cannot touch him." Harper turned in his seat to face toward Grace and rolled his eyes as he said "I got into so much grief when I had him in the frame for a job, nearly five years ago now but he nailed me for harassment. Nearly pushed it to court but they backed down with a payment to charity and a written apology from me. I got hauled over the coals on that and we have kept an eye on him, but if he gets a sniff of surveillance, then we will be back in court for harassment. It was a bit of a miss on my side as we knew we had no evidence that would hold up in court and he has no previous convictions. I just pushed too hard and too often so gave them the harassment case on a plate. And he had a good lawyer. So he is rotten to the core but we need to catch him in the act or get something *really* good to allow us to bug his place or stake him out."

"But you do think he is involved?"

"If it's a local gang. Then he could be."

"Does he live nearby?"

"Yes...but did you hear what I just said, my balls will be on the line if he complains."

"Let's keep your balls out of this but I think we need to rattle a cage or two as we need to think that it's not an inside job. I've never met him and can plead ignorance plus he may not even be in. But let's rattle a cage, we have to start considering an outside job. Let's see what this guy has to say for himself."

28

The Consultant saw the alarm flash to let him know that someone was coming down the drive and went out to meet them. He walked from the porch and it did look to be the police from the car itself (although unmarked) and from those who emerged. He was inwardly pleased to recognise Harper and went as far as to reach out a friendly hand that was shaken.

"DC Harper! This is an unexpected surprise. Is everything all right?"

"Can I introduce DCI Grace." Harper ignored the question and handed the hot potato to Grace who was having the glad hand treatment now.

"It's always good to meet the local constabulary, but I wonder why you are here?" and he did look perplexed. Grace responded.

"There was a burglary this morning in Leckhampton. A safe was opened and items of value were taken. I would like to know if you had anything to do with it?"

The perplexed look morphed into a baffled look and a bit of a chuckle. But he didn't respond, only slowly turning to look over his shoulder towards his house from which a suited man emerged dabbing at his mouth with a napkin looking like he had just been disturbed whilst dining. Harper instantly turned away and eventually did a pirouette whilst groaning and muttering expletives. Grace looked sideways at this strange reaction and wasn't at all sure what was going on. The Consultant provided some clarity for Grace.

"Can I introduce Mr Harvey. He's a friend of mine who was dining with me and he also happens to be my solicitor. Mr Harvey, you will remember DC Harper from before and this is DCI Grace. They are asking me about an incident this morning, they seem to suspect my involvement." No hands were shaken. The solicitor clearly thought he should earn his retainer and addressed Grace with a friendly but direct tone.

"Miss, I can only expect that you are here without knowledge of the injunction for harassment that was lodged with the police by my client and is currently in abeyance? But that assumption is rather doubtful due to the presence of your colleague here. His presence infers that you jolly-well do know that you should not be here harassing my client. It seems very fortuitous that I happen to be dining with my friend to prevent any unpleasantness. Can I ask, and I should warn you to be careful how you respond to this question, why are you here?"

Grace knew that she was on dangerous ground that was covered in thin ice. They had no real suspicion and clearly no warrant; they were there to rattle a cage, but it seems that the table had turned. She gave the pair her best smile.

It was a very good one and they smiled back.

"We dropped in as we were passing and I now think we will carry on passing."

"I think that would be for the best. I think we can all return to what we were doing previously before the disruption." *Phew* thought Harper "I shall, of course, remind the Chief of Policing that the injunction is only in abeyance and ensure she is aware of your visiting *whilst you were passing*." Harper's heart sank and he imagined his balls being twisted by the Chief as he put his hand on Grace's arm to signify a dignified retreat was required.

All Grace could offer was "well it's nice to put faces to names so it was lovely to meet you both and I *do* look forward to meeting again." They turned and walked back to their car and started to head back to town.

"Well, that's my career over, it's been lovely working with you ma'am. You recognised the solicitor?"

"Not at first. But yes I have seen him in action in court. It's OK though, you did warn me, so the fault is mine. But don't you think we just walked into a trap?"

"Yep, there's no luck in that timing. He will be leaving a message for the Chief as we speak and that means we just stuffed our chances of staking that place out or trying to put him through the wringer again."

"We just need to build a case and come back with a warrant and a better reason than 'we were just passing and wondered if you have stolen any diamonds?'"

"That might feel like a step backwards ma'am but he was prepared with his lawyer, he knew we were coming and the news hasn't been out very long. He is in this. I smell it!"

29

It didn't take Grace long to get back to the office

but still found a message to go to see the chief on arrival. Her 'to do' list was already long enough but she couldn't ignore the directive and one of the items she had to clear early was one of demarcation, she wasn't in the robbery squad so would she still be the lead on the case?

Clearly the solicitor was connected enough to get a message to the chief quickly and with enough vim that she became more concerned for her own current rank than covering for Harper. The situation was explained at high volume. It seemed that the force had come close to a court case that would have resulted in the washing and hanging out of lots of dirty laundry on how the force worked when they had a felon in their sights but didn't have previous convictions or hard evidence to back up their suspicions. A large settlement was in the offing but they were let down easy, all out of court and most importantly with little ceremony or fanfare *and* no story in The Echo. However, the police were left being wary of crossing lines with the Consultant again. As the chief came down from the ceiling Grace continued to apologise and repeat that Harper had warned her against the course of action that she unilaterally decided to take and eventually they hit a silence and Grace asked if she should hand the case to the robbery squad. The chief seemed to ponder that but was just making her squirm as she was happy with her competency, despite the moaning and criticism of the past few minutes. She let her go with a grumpy "give me an update on progress at close of play."

The real business then started at the stand-up meeting with the small team in the incident room. Harper and Grace liked these sessions as it brought more people into the discussions, into the circle of ideas and got things done, especially when they had lots of lines of enquiry heading off in many directions at the start of these big jobs.

Grace commenced from the top of her list and

started to tick things off as they went. "Harrison, what's on the CCTV."

"Nothing at all. I went through the night's tape and saw nothing. Very perplexing as everything looks to be working. Looking at the content it's just a night in the office. The security guy is clear he did everything right. He could have been sloppy and not pressed record, but the right tape was in the recorder. It maybe they copied a previous night's tape. But whatever it was; there is no CCTV."

"And the alarms?"

"A bit more there. The fire door..." at this point he rather pointlessly pointed to a glossy picture of the door on the incident board "triggered an alarm at 22:10. It was active for twenty five seconds. The alarm supplier did nothing as it was so short. They said it would have been on and off their screens before anyone noticed. The same alarm was triggered at 2:10 and for thirty-eight seconds this time. The alarm company did then take notice and they rang it in. Our operations desk took the call at 2:12 but we took no action at our end as we had no notes on the business and were told the alarm had stopped."

"We didn't cover ourselves in glory there. We better keep that gem quiet. OK so crap alarm and no CCTV. Has SOCO got anything?

"Not a great deal, but that speaks volumes in-itself. Whoever did this had overshoes and cleaned up after themselves, literally polished off any prints including the staff and families'. SOCO were quite pleased as it gave them less to do. They went all over the place and found nothing. But that does mean we know what they touched as they cleaned the VCR and the toolbox by the door" at this point there was more pointing at another glossy photo "and there was plenty of activity by the toolbox and the fire door. Now that's important as the business doesn't use this

106

door, they enter via the roller doors, so the trails in the dust are likely to be our villain's. There are also some tyre tracks of an SUV, Range Rover type most likely. They have fibres and hair that they are comparing to the known staff but I cannot say we are hopeful."

"Anything from the house to house?"

Harrison shook his head and drew in his lips before saying "the closest house is fifty yards away and they heard and saw nothing. I tried the alarm myself and it could hardly be heard from outside their house. No other CCTV nearby from other businesses that cover this building either."

Grace summed up the situation whilst turning to look at the incident board that didn't actually have much on it "so a great, big, nothing, so far on hard evidence. Harper; thoughts?"

"Well…" said Harper putting down his coffee and scratching his jaw "they were inside for four hours. If they had the keys and combination and took time to wipe everything down they could have been in and out in an hour. So they took their time as they needed to pick locks and crack the safe. I have had a chat with our technicians and some of the locks are better than others and the safe is a good one…doing them all in four hours was thought to be very optimistic but perhaps they were good and perhaps they were lucky. So how did they get in. It looks like they opened the door and walked in and we know the door they used and as it only opens from the inside it must have been opened from someone on the inside. And the footprints in the dust point to someone hiding by that toolbox."

"Or in it?" offered Harrison tentatively.

"Let's get it open and find out" suggested Grace and Harrison gave a thumbs up and wrote an action. "So, before we go too far down the new suspect line…did we find anything out from the family statements?"

PC Barker chimed in at that point with her rather lovely Welsh valleys accent, Harper always hoped she would break into song. "Nothing revelatory. Very consistent, lots of alibis some husband to wife alibis but on the whole I didn't smell a rat."

"And a statement from the security guard?"

"Yep, his account stacks up with an alibi from his wife and nothing in his past or bank accounts that looks odd. Apart from he is well paid for being a security guy, but he readily admits that himself."

"And anything on their accounts yet?"

"Yes. I think we know Challen from the SFO" there were nods and grunts of agreement of the recognition of a rather formidable lady from the Serious Fraud Office, "she had a look at the files and dialled into the preliminary interview, it seemed in depth to me and went off into acronyms after about thirty seconds and after about half an hour she said she would look at the accounts in detail. I had a chat with her later and she hasn't found anything at fault. Her words we 'they sail close to the wind when it comes to family trusts' and she means that they pile money into those for tax purposes, but then they have plenty of money. Challen thinks it ties up, they buy cheap and sell high…consistently. Have done for years. So they have ways to…hang on I will use her words again 'mitigate tax'. They have lots of cash in bank. I couldn't see a need to generate cash through a fake robbery and Challen cannot see fraud. They have detailed records of purchases. You asked me to check that boss and it really does look like they had bought diamonds that were in the safe."

"So that's all lovely too then" added Grace as she pulled her hands down her cheeks in some exasperation. Those gathered were looking to her for inspiration and direction but all she saw were avenues closing. They would have to look around for more avenues and start to spiral out from the current suspects. Grace had to rally the troops and started to think aloud.

"Two fundamentals here. They had diamonds. They have been stolen. Very few people seem to have known what was on the premises and if it's not the family stealing from themselves it will be someone close to them, their contacts, employees, people they deal with. We have that list and need to go through it and pull on some leads. It looks like someone was inside and opened the door to let the rest of the gang in. Most likely, it was someone who should have been there and they just hid out in one of the offices or meeting rooms, so let's not close out the inside job yet. But if this *isn't* an inside job then it will be a team that knows locks and safes. If we start local and then get the National Crime Agency's ideas on who it could be. But my feel is that it's locals as they took their time, cleaned up and covered their tracks. They had something to hide. So I think we will hit a nexus, someone who knew, or had a suspicion of diamonds in there and someone who could crack a safe." She paused looking at the incident board for inspiration and Harper continued her point.

"Or they had someone who could draw a team together and find a door opener and a safe opener."

"And if it's a local job then the Consultant could be that person, but we will need a lot more before we go up that driveway again. Let's run through all those connected to DJD and Harper can look through his little black book or wrong-uns for a safe cracker. Harrison, good work so far. Can you look into where I would sell five million pounds of uncut diamonds. We need to start thinking that we try to catch them at the other end of this trail." That was like an admission of failure.

30

The De Jong family were covering the same ground. They had rung all their associates that worked in the same way as their window cleaner, those who periodically received a parcel through the post and brought them to their office. First up was the fact that they made contact, then they didn't beat about the bush in stating that the family wanted to know where they were last night as the police might ask the same question. They were reminded not to mention the packages and this lucrative business would be back to normal soon. In the meantime they could keep sending in their invoices and they would be paid. It didn't take long to track down two who were missing. Glazier, of course, and their gardener, but he had said he would be on holiday and was due to return shortly. He hadn't had a package in a while, whereas Glazier had been there on the day of the robbery. They went to his house and all but broke in. Knocked the door and looked in the windows. No van. All deserted. Their prime suspect.

Their other avenue was to get the family to hit all their own business contacts (from old and nearly forgotten to well-known connections) to get the word out. They set out with the aim to ensure that you couldn't sell their diamonds in Europe or the east coast of America without them knowing. That may sound difficult, but it is a closed market to try to prevent blood diamonds and embargoed countries selling diamonds. People tended to deal with sources, suppliers and people they knew. And this was a large amount of diamonds.

They also had another strand and everyone they talked to they offered a reward. They asked their insurance company to attend an urgent meeting and a loss adjuster duly arrived and they set out their stall. They needed their five million sum insured ready as they didn't expect the police to find their diamonds. The police will waste time looking inwards at the family but it was the family that would find, through their contacts, who was trying to sell the diamonds and they could reward that tip off and potentially buy their diamonds back for a lot less than five million. This could be enticing for the insurer as the alternative was to pay all of the five million sum insured and DJD would buy new stock and effectively start from scratch. The family preferred plan A and the loss adjuster also had a preference to that as it would reduce their loss. He would continue to look at all aspects of the loss carefully and he departed to do just that.

The family wearily came back to the de facto board room table in dribs and drabs as their phone work ground to a halt. They talked in ones and twos and then papa De Jong suggested a take-away and they came together to sort the order. A daughter left to dial-in the request and as silence fell papa closed the meeting.

"So, we keep at this tomorrow with anyone we have missed. Our best chance it to see where they come back onto the market. We need to get them all back before anyone else can get a look at them. Anyone in the know will see it's more than five million pounds worth and questions will follow and that will be the business finished. We need to keep close to the police. They will get onto that window cleaner soon and will be better placed to track him but I know someone we can talk to. Someone who may know who could put a team together to rob us." He looked up a number in his little black book and texted the Consultant.

31

The news had broken. Glazier and the Consultant checked the news channels as each one tried to outdo the other on the story and then it was clear that cameras had appeared on scene and presenters stood on the road in which they had been travelling only hours before. At first it was vague news of a high value robbery but as the news circulated it was clear that sources and informants were found (or paid) and the truth began to seep out like a crack in a dam and then it was out. This was the biggest robbery in the southwest in years with five million pounds of diamonds being stolen from DJD. Other sources picked it up and soon it was 'in excess of five million' and was likely to keep growing. A talking head appeared from the industry to state that such businesses would keep a low profile and would often forgo security firms with armoured vans for personally couriering diamonds worth large sums, often overseas, on their own person and rely on anonymity over overt security. The expert did elucidate on the process of buying, grading, refining and selling and confirmed "that, within the industry, DJD was known as a longstanding and reliable part of the wholesale diamond market."

Eventually, they turned from the unfolding reports and Glazier was ecstatic at the news. "Five million, that's massive. We'll all be set for life. Surely you are happy with that?" he looked quizzically at the Consultant who looked far from happy. Why hadn't he found out what DJD were involved in himself; his 'intelligence' network had let him down. He stood and paced but soon realised that knowing wouldn't have changed much. He would have ended up where he was now, with multiple millions of diamonds to sell.

"It's a massive coup. We've pulled off the biggest robbery in the town. But now we have to get away with it. Shifting such a large amount of…" and he wondered if he should be honest here and decided to be "…something that I have never handled before isn't going to be easy. I'm not sure where to start. I don't know the market at all, I have done a few in the past up to a guy in the Birmingham Jewellery Quarter but this is a different scale." He was a bit lost, the scale made his task all the more difficult. What the hell did he plan to do? He decided he was hungry. "I'll make sausage and mash and you see what you can find out about the diamond market."

32

Grace and Harper had returned to the scene of the crime. It was a lot busier than their morning call with onlookers, police and press in attendance. The chief had been briefed and made an empty holding statement and then put pressure on Grace to get a result. During all this Harper had stepped away to take a call. "The De Jong family have been on the phone, they cannot track down their window cleaner. They have *suggested* that he could look into the building when cleaning the windows. Seems a bit odd to me as they seem to be pointing the finger based on that, but I did ask when they last saw him and he cleaned the windows the same day the robbery occurred."

"Ahh, that's interesting so ties in with our thought that someone came and hid out till later." They were stood by the fire door and looked about expecting the hiding place to be obvious; and it kind of was. "So, marks in the dust here around the egress and ingress point and around that toolbox." Harper liked Grace using words like *egress* in conversation and had a look at the toolbox she was pointing at, he lifted the lid and pulled out drawers. Most slid with difficulty. "All the contents seem to have slid to the back. Look, there are places for the individual spanners but they have all fallen to the back of the drawer, like the thing has been tilted."

"Or placed on its back?" They both took hold of it and laid it on its back, had a look at the base then up ended it again and Harper had a look inside again.

"But why would they do that? Why lie it down? OK, perhaps it was moved and taken away." They looked at one-another with a quizzical expression waiting for the other to come up with an idea.

"So the window cleaner was here and left before the place was locked up and perhaps that toolbox was taken away…perhaps another was left in its place" Grace was warming to this theory "do you think they could have a similar looking toolbox, close enough for the security guard not to notice a difference and hide someone inside it?" Harper had a long look.

"They could have. But it wouldn't be me, or you, someone small or a child, but they could hide in a pretend toolbox, come out later and open the fire door. I know! There was a wooden horse, in a film. Had Brad Pitt in it."

"The Aeneid by Virgil."

"I don't think it was called that." Grace smiled warmly at Harper and explained. "No, I was referring to the poem by Virgil where he talked about the Trojan war and the Trojan Horse."

"That's what I meant, but there wasn't poetry in this film. Lots of swords and sandals…but we are off point. The point is they could have hidden someone in another toolbox and have had to move the real one and that resulted in everything inside being moved about."

"But why switch this one back, that would have taken some time?" Harper had an answer to that.

"They took longer to leave. That always niggled me and perhaps this is why. They wanted to take away their Trojan Horse box. It would be a good lead and have forensics perhaps. It's just covering tracks and it has left us scratching our heads. Perhaps it's just to mess with us."

"Well, I think it's a sound theory. They used someone small for sure. Do you know any local, short, safe crackers?"

114

"No. I know an old, normal sized, one. And I have news on that. I had to have a bit of a dig about as he has been very quiet for some years. His name is Tom Davis and was on trial for conspiracy. There was a grass who pointed the finger in his direction and we should have had him serving a longer sentence, but as part of the parole and the haggle over doing time he cleared out his workshop and tools so he has retired. But he was good and certainly could have a look at an old, but tricky safe like they had. I have asked about and sent a car to bring him in for a chat but he isn't at home. Neighbours say he has a house abroad and he and his wife are off there. They say they have been gone a while. I will check it out myself as it seems a little too coincidental them going away just before this and want to see if the neighbours are sure they both went at the same time and if they drove, flew or whatever. Is a passport check OK after I have had a look into it?"

"Yes, of course. It does sound too much of a coincidence. Check if the De Jongs know the guy at all? That's a long shot, but we seem to have the window cleaner to look into too. Let's knock on some doors and pull the stops out on finding those two. Blinky Harper, we seem to have suspects all of a sudden!"

33

The Consultant was at the sink and looking down his driveway and he didn't like what he saw. The kid's father was approaching at some speed. He pulled up sharply by the back door and the Consultant dried his hands and handed the spud peeling task onto Glazier. The kid's father stepped out and stood waiting at the bonnet of the car as his child moved gingerly from the passenger seat a bruise over her left eye. The Consultant knew what a beaten child looked like and this was one. The child hung her head and trudged after her father whilst the door was knocked loudly. From the outset the Consultant feared how this would end and steeled himself to being placatory. He opened the porch door and stepped back indicating that, keys etc should be deposited and this was grudgingly done and the Consultant took close notice of the metal detector as the father was shown into the living room. He hadn't brought his phone with him.

The Consultant blocked the kid's way. "You can help Glazier in the kitchen. Sausages for tea if you're lucky" and he indicated the way that she should go. He could hear Glazier opening up a chat and getting the child involved as he shut the kitchen door. The Consultant took a breath and followed the father, closing the dining room door behind himself. The kid's father was stalking about the room, head bowed, glowering, fists clenched. The Consultant mirrored none of this, stood straight pulled out a seat at the baize covered card table and sat gesturing that they should both sit. Nothing had yet been said, there would be a monologue, one that was practiced and fiery to start proceedings.

"Five million pounds in uncut diamonds" a finger was jabbed toward the fireplace as the pacing continued "you must think I'm a mug. I'm not going to sit around and wait for you and your mates to piss off to Marbella" he turned to face the Consultant for the first time and spat out a question with his teeth bared "do you think I'm stupid?"

The Consultant thought that could be rhetorical but didn't offer any answer and stared back and it didn't take long for the performance to recommence. "I found it all out. You tried to turn my own kid against me, but I have found it all out. Everything! Where you went, how you did it and your little names for each other. Safe, sparks, or whatever and you as the leader." The jabbed finger had turned to the Consultant "and you are planning to freeze me out of it…I told you that I want my cut now. I'm not taking your crap about waiting…waiting for you all to piss off with five million diamonds." He came over to the table but not with the intention of sitting, he just wanted to be more threatening. "Are you going to say anything?"

The response was intended to be calming, a low voice, only their eyes being locked suggested the undertone of malice "I cannot add anything to what I said before. You saw the news and now you know who was involved, but the situation is unchanged, I don't have cash to give you. You will have to wait…" and at this he saw the agitation rise and the kid's father turned away in frustration at hearing what he didn't want to listen to "…wait and trust me. You will get what is due to you. That's the way I work. It is all on trust, no-one says anything, we all work together and we all trust one another. You are inside the circle now. You placed yourself there so you need to keep our secret. Omerta. You understand? You betray no-one. Ever. And for me I always need to pay what's due; that's why your kid is getting a full cut in the first place. But be sure where you are now, in the circle and secrecy is sacrosanct."

"Words, words, words! They don't pay the bills and I *don't* trust you. I *don't* know or like you so don't think that I am bound by your pact. I know I'm not inside your circle. I have seen nothing that makes me think that you are not going to run with my cash" and at that he finally came and sat down, slouched and leaning backwards with tightly folded arms in a defiant pose "you're going to run and leave me looking like a twat and I'm not going to take that. You need to pay me." There was silence but the Consultant could see where this was heading and made a pre-emptive strike.

"Be careful what you say next. I told you that you can trust me and I will pay you, just not yet." A smile spread over the kid's father's face.

"You are scared. You know that I have you by the balls. I'm not in your circle. I am so outside of it" he warmed to his theme "you need to pay me or I will tell the police what I know."

The Consultant inhaled through his nose. It had happened. The threat had been made again. The second time. "I want a million. I will take two hundred and fifty thousand this week, otherwise…" the consultant cut him off.

"No! Don't threaten me again. I have warned you twice already. I have given you two chances but don't go pushing my buttons" he tried to remain calm but his buttons had been pushed and he shuffled in his chair and leaned forward narrowing the gap between them but kept his stare level, even and intense and moved his hands onto his knees so that he had an open posture. "Three chances are more than I give to others but don't push me, so you beat the truth out of your kid, well done big man, changes nothing, you don't get more than the others and you don't get anything before the others. You are the same as the others, you wait *and you say nothing. Understand? Nothing!*"

This was the moment. The kid's father had to back down and he pondered his options. He took a while, kept glowering but despite the inflamed look he lowered his voice and said "you seem rattled. I do have the upper hand. My offer stands. Two hundred and fifty this week" and then he smiled, trying to look relaxed, still with arms folded. Happy that he had seemingly won.

"And if I don't?"

"Well then I will go to the police."

The Consultant exhaled with some resignation and his expression changed, his brow furrowed, his eyes narrowed, his lips drew back so his teeth were bared and a face reappeared. It was the face he presented when he had been pushed into a corner. Such corners as he had been in before. This is a face that few saw, those in a school playground, those in his children's home, those in the forces with him and those facing him in other dark days that he tried hard to forget, it was the face he used when he had been cornered and realised that his only real option is to come out fighting. He had also learnt that when fighting he needed to use overwhelming violence. The kid's father saw the change and realised he had pushed too far and too hard, but it was too late.

"I warned you. I told you three times not to threaten me. You had three chances." The Consultant kept a small revolver concealed below the card table for encounters such as this and he then pulled his right hand above the tabletop and without hesitation levelled the revolver at the kid's father's forehead and immediately pulled the trigger.

It was a loud bang for a small room, plenty of smoke, a hole erupted between the eyes of the kid's father and his head was pushed back, his body slumped and then tumbled forward and there was a large thud as his head hit the green baize. The Consultant folded the baize over the corpses head, bunching it to keep the gore and blood wadded within the absorbent fabric as he worked to stop any blood oozing to the floor. He also just wanted not to see what he had done, to literally cover it up. As he did this he stated with annoyance to the room that had so recently had two lives within it "three times. I warned you."

Glazier appeared at the door, he stood on the threshold, hand on the doorknob and not sure what to do as a look of surprise and indecision covered his face. The Consultant swivelled in his seat, his visage had reverted to its normal bearing and looked up as the kid also entered to see her father slumped, covered and dead; and to see her father's killer. The Consultant needed to be directive and make swift moves to fix and conceal this.

"He was blackmailing us all. He wanted cash or would

go to the police. I tried to reason with him, but he didn't trust me and I don't trust him. You both" he gestured in their direction "I do absolutely trust. This isn't about loose ends, this is about trust." He looked at the child in the room "Glazier and I can see, and your dad told me, that he beat you to tell him what he wanted. You couldn't help that. He was your father. But he shouldn't have put you in that position. But we will look after you now Kid. I hold the responsibility and I think Glazier and I will agree to look after you from now on. We are not going to see you suffer cos your dad couldn't keep shtum. Glazier, if you and the kid want to take off, if you don't feel safe then I understand. I'm going to clean all this up and it will take some time. If you think this..." he looked over the corpse and the room where smoke hung in the air, the smell of blood and cordite mingled, it was a catastrophe "is going to happen to you two then head off. But this isn't what I do. I did try to avoid it. He just wouldn't listen and I couldn't risk him taking all of us down." He continued to be seated as he didn't like the task ahead of him, but he knew he needed to clean up his mess. He asked Glazier to look after the kid and keep to the kitchen while he cleaned the room and then he would be outside for some time. If he could feed the kid then all the better and there would be school tomorrow; consistency and acting as normal as possible was still the key and he suggested putting some arnica on the kid's face.

The Consultant didn't take on jobs that involved body disposal and he had not had to do this task for some years; many years ago he had been trained to kill within the UK forces, switch on and act then switch off. As a civilian he could use extreme force but over the years he had had to resort to this less and less. He had never got used to death, but he had become more used to the disposal process.

He had a sack truck in the barn and the chair and the

still covered body were strapped to that as a unit and taken into the barn. The chair was connected to the hoist above the metal shredder. Here the Consultant donned headphones and turned the music up loud. He had learned from experience that the less he saw and heard from now on the better for his sanity. The body was released from the chair and tumbled with a reverberating thud into the hopper, the green baize trailing behind like a cape. All his own clothes then followed and he went into a Tyvek suit. He returned to the house with wipes and bleach and wiped down surfaces and was pleased that there was not much to do. For that domestic pistol he used only low-pressure, round-nose bullets, to try to prevent having to dig rounds out of walls or having to have too much to clean up. He took a view that he could always use more bullets if one had not been enough. He ejected the magazine from the gun and removed the bullets. He would lock those in the store in the barn and the pistol and all the cleaning cloths he used were bagged and went into the hopper to be shredded. The hopper was then covered in a plastic sheet to catch and contain spray and then after increasing the volume on his headphone again, he turned the shredder on. Even through the music he could feel and remember the noise. He walked away and fired up the furnace and paced the room until he thought enough time had passed and he then lowered an old mattress into the shredder and it bore down on the plastic cover and was taken into the shredder. The mattress shuddered and jolted within the hopper as it was gripped, pulled and mangled. Its wadding and stuffing cleaned the machine as it carried all before it and absorbed the worst of the gore. The Consultant then climbed the gantry at the side of the hopper and sluiced it down with a pressure washer.

All the shredded material was then placed into the furnace. It would need a slow, hot burn, but there was plenty to clean up in the meantime. The Tyvek suit went in and was replaced again, a new baize cover was placed on the table, the chair was meticulously cleaned and put back in place and when he finally checked the furnace, very little was left. Steel from the bed springs was puddling at the base of the furnace. He tapped that into a poor ingot and turned the furnace off and headed inside for a shower and to see if Glazier had decided to stick around. He had. The kid had been subdued and worried, they both had been, but they had all seemed to return to some form of new reality and that did mean that no-one was planning to run away. They made a plan for the morning. It would be an early start, they would take the kid's father's car back to his house. The kid would get off to school and then be brought back to the Consultant's place after school. Glazier and the Consultant would sort everything out at the house, there was a list of things to find and sort. Lots to think about to clear up this mess. And that was enough for the day. The Consultant retired to bed and lay looking at the ceiling trying to clear his mind of the sights, sounds and smells of the day. He had solved nothing, problems swirled and now he had an orphan to look after.

34

Harper reported that their suspects had vanished. They had knocked on various doors and contacted other agencies and talked to the De Jongs and found nothing tangible...so that was significant. The potential safe cracker was not at his home. It was clear that he had a place in Europe but trying to find where was proving elusive. They had a warrant and entered his house, which was difficult as clearly the security of his own home was rather good. They found a house that did look like it had been left as people were going away. Everything was turned off apart from the freezer, fridge propped open, bleach in the sink and toilets. They left a constable to find paperwork for their foreign base, but without much hope. This all seemed very prepared...they had gone and the wife's passport had been used to fly to Lisbon but the safe cracker's hadn't.

The window cleaner was similar but less clean or thorough and that indicated that if he was running he had no intention of returning. He was gone for good. His was a rented flat, his van was outside and they had forensics go over the whole place only to find nothing of interest. He had worked with the De Jongs and there were invoices and cash in the bank that matched up. For both suspects there was a deep probe into backgrounds and known associates of a dubious sort.

The safe guy was a professional criminal with a suspected long history but only one crime proven. He had eventually been caught in a warehouse robbery when the whole gang had been swept up by one of their number turning informant. He had served three years and there was a long break of retirement until this job. The window cleaner had been a young offender with a list of crime long enough and severe enough to get him before the wrong (or right) magistrate and then he had served time too. But that short-sharp-shock had seemed to lead to reform until this job. They had no link, other than living in the same town and now being in the frame for the same job.

"What's your thoughts Harps?" it was time for a coffee and muffin at Waterstones cafe. They were sat on the first-floor veranda overlooking London plane trees and the Promenade with its restaurants and gentle bustle towards House of Fraser. A busker was covering any Boots corner road noise with something that could once have been by Vivaldi.

"I think they are part of the team. The window cleaner saw, or knew something from being there, perhaps he saw the safe and got the safe cracker involved, not that we can see a link between them. I've got to say though that he was well paid for cleaning windows, you'd think he was good at it, but he was doing it every month."

"So, you think he was being paid for something else?"

"I'm not sure I go with the altruistic De Jong family spending loads on sparkling windows; sure they have lots of cash, but seems an odd way to spend it, overpaying for clean windows."

"He came and went regularly doing some favours for the family…and the security guy said he was certainly there on the day of the crime. Do you think he made the Trojan toolbox?"

Harper pondered, "the safe cracker had more of a workshop for making stuff. And more space at his house as they took the toolbox with them didn't they. So, if one of those two had taken it then wouldn't we have found it at their places, or in his van? No, there are more involved. The little guy…"

"Person" interjected Grace.

"Person" repeated Harper "and the tyre treads were for an SUV not the window cleaner's transit. Plus nothing from our two delinquents' past has them as the planner for something like this. I keep circling back to the Consultant pulling a team in that included someone" and Harper counted them on his fingers "who could open safes, was small enough to be in the Trojan toolbox and the window guy who suggested this thing." He stopped for a bite of triple chocolate muffin.

Grace took a sip and put her coffee down and looked up into the weak sun for some warmth and provided her thoughts "and potentially another for muscle or redundancy as suggested by the forensics. So let's go for five as they had people to carry out the diamonds and the Trojan toolbox in such quick time but they all fit into one car."

Good point thought Harper and Grace followed it up with another, "and where do you buy a Trojan toolbox?" Good question thought Harper and stopped mid bite and nodded in appreciation then continued to munch.

"You would need a donor toolbox (we can look into that) then you knock it about to remove all the inside bits and then disguise it as an old one. I'm sorry to say that I don't think that's overly difficult, lots of people could do it…but there may not be many of the donor toolboxes around. The security guard said it had been there for years. I will get someone to have a look at it all."

They both drank and finished their muffin crumbs and sat in what was left of that year's sun facing the issue that they didn't really have anywhere to go next. Grace summed up.

"We have suspects that are in the wind. We have the Consultant in the frame, potentially, but nothing to link him to this job other than he's a wrong un. The De Jongs seem to be swimming in money, probably too much money and they really want their diamonds back and we have our hopes pinned on finding a toolbox. I really hope they don't sell them in Argos and there are thousands of them." She leaned forward with her elbows on the table and pushed her hands through her hair and talked down to the tabletop "we don't have much Harps." She still had her head in her hands as Harper took an upbeat assessment.

"But we will get them. They have five million pounds of diamonds to move. They might as well have the crown jewels. As soon as they try to do something to move it we will get them. The word is out far-and-wide to look out for a sniff of dodgy diamonds. This might be the long game boss. Patience."

"Fine for you to say. Don't you plan to retire in two-years?"

"Oh I meant the long game for you! I'm not

postponing my retirement for anyone."

35

The Consultant arrived at The Beehive and took his normal seat when his solicitor came, ordered some food and drink and then sat down.

"I want to buy a house." The solicitor snorted in response and then looked pleased.

"It would be good to do something normal for you for once, I'm normally playing interference with the police, so very happy to charge my extortionate rates for some conveyancing. Do you have a place in mind?" An envelope was passed.

"So that's got the address and details of the estate agent. It also contains the passport, ID and some bills for the guy who is selling it and his bank details. He won't be around to sign anything as he has left the country." There was a pause and an inhalation that coincided with a steak sandwich appearing from the kitchen. The pair had worked together long enough to know that the owner had left more than the country.

"I knew it was too good to believe."

"You can sort the sale, put the proceeds in the account?"

"Eminently doable, clearly with some bending of rules, but that's what you pay me for. Do you need it quickly."

"Not at all. The house owner will pass on the proceeds to his daughter, her details are in there too. He knows that he will be travelling for some time and she will need the proceeds in the future. Sort the purchase then move the house contents into storage and then from storage to a house clearance place after a year."

"So literally clearing house then."

"Yes, but there's a child involved and I am going to look

after her. Like a ward."

"Oh?" The solicitor was shocked…and for a man in his position he was *very* difficult to shock. He settled back into the settle and took some beer and looked out of the window for a moment and pulled a frown. "Well. Am I giving parenting advice now too?"

"You may have to." The Consultant still was frustrated at the turn of events and rolled back in his mind to the mistake he had made in getting the girl involved and then making himself master of her destiny. Here he was planning her future. He decided to stay honest "it was a mess up on my behalf I shouldn't have involved this girl and her dad in something and the wheel has fallen off and I am responsible. I would want you to meet her. Your wife and girls would be good for her, she has no-one now. I plan to send her to board at Ladies' College so knowing your two may help smooth that path."

"Are you serious?" the solicitor asked that gently, in a probing way, not as an accusation or criticism and leaned in and lowered his voice, not that he was overly worried about a client and solicitor being bugged "with all that you have going on, you are bringing a child into your life?"

"I have burned my bridges on this. I made a mistake and should try and fix it." He looked intently at his friend. One of the very few people that knew, at least some of, the scope of the life he leads. His eyes betrayed his sadness. "I know something of being an orphan, I'm not leaving the kid to the state to care for. I will do what I can to help her and if she resents me for the rest of my life then I will understand. If we get on and do live together then yes, she will know all that I have going on and we will see what happens."

His friend reached out and patted his upper arm, about as close to an emotional response as they were ever likely to share "well all the girls will be happy to help as we can and I can sort any legalities in due course. If it helps my wife and kids all hate me at differing points of the day and I haven't done anything to offend them, other than breathing and being a breadwinner. Is there a cover-story in place?"

"Yes, father is an old friend from the military. He has taken a job offshore on oil rigs. Well paid, but weeks away so boarding school and a solicitor with power of attorney to sort things while he is away. He will sort out a house up-north at some point. Her mother died just a few years ago so she has no-one."

"And you can get her into the Ladies' College?"

"Oh yes. I have a favour to call in there. The headmistress owes me for a delicate matter I sorted very swiftly for them. She will be in as a day boarder in short order. I won't ask for a discount on the fees and will make a suitable donation to something arty."

They arranged to introduce the girls later in the weekend and then the lunch was up and the solicitor covered off other items of business being progressed within his retainer, had a general gossip and then left.

***

The Consultant checked his watch and thought about calling it a day. Someone had texted asking for a repeat of a prior job and he had stated where they could meet, but after the events of yesterday, he wasn't feeling himself and thought of leaving. But being back in 'normal' surroundings waiting to see what jobs would come his way whilst reading a book, and having a beer in The Beehive, did at least let him relax.

A man began to approach. He was well dressed his subtly impressive shirt was then beaten by the jacket and trousers that were well tailored and matching but not as a suit would, it was more casual but had elan. He had a very

nice Rolex, not golden and diamond encrusted, again a subtle expensive touch. Diamonds were in his gold cufflinks. He wasn't overweight, was tanned and had his thinning dark hair smoothed back. His earlier good looks had faded through time, he must be past his sixties, but his style added attraction. But there was an issue. He held a glass of orange juice in both hands and he looked ill at ease, not to the state of a claustrophobic in this busy bar, but you got the feeling that this man was not used to being in a pub. He spotted the news and sporting papers and came over bringing with him a musky odour. The guy even smelt good.

The Consultant took on his normal, non-committal air of a friendly welcome and then returned to his Partick O'Brian.

"We've talked in the past" offered the stranger as an opener, "many years ago. You looked into someone's background for me. An unofficial check before employment. You did a very thorough job. We didn't meet or even share our names. All via email. I liked the discretion. You were kind enough to let me have your number and I have kept it all these years."

This was reassuring if they had worked together in the distant past then there was a good chance that this approach wasn't of too much concern. "Do you need another background check?" that line of business had dried up with the advent of CRB checks but the Consultant's checks could go well beyond the information that a CRB could provide.

"No. I have been robbed."

The Consultant pulled a face in mock anguish "well I am sorry to hear that, but I am not sure a refund is due, you said that this recruitment was some time ago?"

"I know it wasn't the person you checked out. They are still in my employ." The old man kept both hands on his

129

undrunk orange juice but turned his body to the Consultant and gave him his full attention and closed out the rest of the pub whilst lowering his voice.

"I want you to get back what was taken from me."

The Consultant had had such approaches in the past and he was aware that a crew were busy in the Worcestershire-Gloucestershire border doing house robberies. Making mischief with antiques. A long case clock could be difficult to sell if it had unusual features and a run-of-the-mill one wasn't worth much, unless it had sentimental value to the owner. Then there was a happy symmetry, a lovely arbitrage that could be taken advantage of; the buyer would pay over the odds, the seller take less than market value and the Consultant could make money at both ends and still make both parties happy, the seller as a difficult piece was sold and the buyer had their heirloom back. And it was easy, the piece was left for collection and money changed hands without anyone meeting; but it had to be worth-while as the Consultant would only make pence in the pound.

"That may be possible. Can I ask what has been taken?"

"Five million pounds worth of diamonds. I want them all back."

This was a real test for the Consultant. He prided himself on his poker face, worked hard on showing no emotions at all and at this time the best thing he could do was to take a slow swig of beer to hide his face for a few seconds and let his mind consider what was happening. Had he been found out? Was this guy fishing? Who the hell was he? With so many questions he had no response so he was glad that the old man continued. "I have little faith in the police. I think you may have inside channels, a network if you like. You may be able to use those channels to get my diamonds back."

The Consultant did a calculation on whether this guy could be trusted at all and decided that he couldn't be.

"I've seen this story in the news. It's big news so I cannot help you. The police are all over this. If I was able to help then the police would only want to know how you mysteriously found what was missing. Your insurers too, I saw that they offered a reward. They would be like a dog with a bone if they think they paid out *and* you got your stuff back. And you know me of old and remember my rules. Complete secrecy so I couldn't be asking too many questions on who did this and then tell you who it was. If diamonds are offered to me, then I would be surprised as it's not something I know about. Metals are my thing, consulting on other matters perhaps; but you lost a large amount of diamonds, I don't think they will come my way."

The stranger looked a mixture of perplexed and angry. "So you know that there is a sizeable reward?"

"Claiming rewards is not in my psyche" explained the Consultant "I wouldn't tell the police if my *enemy* did this robbery, it would end anyone's trust in me; and talking of trust, can I ask your interest in this?" The talk of insurance and rewards had led the Consultant to consider if the person he was dealing with was a representative of the insurer, a loss adjuster, or freelancer looking to recover the goods. With a smooth and practiced move the stranger revealed who he was through the production of a business card from his breast pocket. As business cards went it was a good one. You couldn't help yourself from running your thumb over the card and feeling the heft of the card and the embossed print and turning it over in your hand. The obverse had a photo of a cut diamond on a bed of black velvet, it was well lit and was working as a prism. A rather lovely image. The opposite side stated papa De Jong's name, his email and that he was chairman of De Jong's diamonds plc. No address was provided. The Consultant took a moment and placed the card into his wallet and tucked that away and awaited the next move. Had he been rumbled or was this just co-incidental and De Jong was trying to reach-out to someone from his past who could help? De Jong was intently looking at his juice, this didn't feel like he was trying to strong arm his diamonds back. This all piqued the curiosity of the Consultant and he decided to push a bit.

"Can I ask something? The insurer is involved and should pay out. Why would you want your goods back if you are indemnified through their payment?" There was no response other than both men looking intently at one another and then the penny dropped for the Consultant "unless you don't get indemnity. The claim amount does not actually cover what you have lost, you must be underinsured." They both nodded gently at this truth. The diamonds were insured for five million but their worth was more, much more perhaps. The Consultant did what he does and gave some advice. "I can see two immediate problems. If you do find who had your goods and you get them back the insurer will want their payout back. You cannot have their money and the diamonds, insurance does not work that way. And the police will be all over it, they would want to know how you retrieved your goods and, although you are the victim of crime, start looking at you for perverting the course of justice or wasting police time or even parking fines, they wouldn't be happy that you solved your own crime. So take the insurance money." He ended with a shrug and the old man looked into his juice once more.

"Perhaps you are right. Perhaps the police will catch them. And I do think that I will see my diamonds again, *if* they come onto the market. It's such a small market. They will pop up, they are effectively unsaleable." He smiled affably and made those shuffling moves as he prepared to leave and with a polite raise of the hand he left. The Consultant looked at the ceiling and now he knew what he had to do. He finished his pint and smiled as the end was in sight…but there were still many challenges ahead.

36

Glazier and the Kid had been busy researching the diamond game. Idle hands and all that. He had taken a paternal and protecting view of the child and was trying to keep her positive and happy whilst being in proximity to the person who had killed her father. He tried to set out an optimistic view, the Kid would be well looked after, she would be provided for financially but that covered the practical aspects and skipped the paternal and maternal unconditional love gap in her life. The Kid hadn't been one to talk much before becoming an orphan, so Glazier had his work cut out but was able to get her to chat. It was clear that life at home had taken a bad turn from her mother's passing. This latest loss wasn't the one that she mourned. Between the Consultant and Glazier they set out a happy path, a green, flower strewn path, where the Kid could grow up happy, with art and mechanics and lots of opportunity to be what she wanted. Some of that was true, favours were called in and she would board at The Ladies' College, everything would be provided for and requests relayed that additional art instruction should be given and the college were told that 'not fitting in' wasn't an option; but there was reassurance there, the school would manage that. The Kid did consider that life at home with two villains was interesting, the workshops and grounds gave more freedom than their old semi and her life wasn't filled with life-long friends anyway. She could move on.

Glazier and the Kid had a task set and that was to try to understand more of what was going on with this stash of diamonds. As part of that Glazier had passed on all he knew and told the story of how he had met the Consultant and how the job had come together. Additionally, they also now knew that the diamonds were worth more than they were insured for. It was the Kid that found a key part of the puzzle. It was the tins that did it. Glazier told her that detail, that the safe had contained tins that looked like bean tins, with no labels, just numbers printed onto the metal and that provoked a memory.

They ate together. Pasta parcels, with cheesecake and squirty aerosol cream for afters and Glazier prompted the Kid to tell what she had found. It was the most that the Kid had ever said in one go within their earshot and they both listened and gently prompted as needed.

"I saw a program on TV. It was about diamond mining, but it was on a ship and the program was about the ship. One built for that purpose and that's what interested me. It was a dredger, pulling up gravel from the sea and then the ship sorted through the gravel and separated the pebbles from the diamonds, or it tried to. That was the impressive part, sieving out what wasn't needed and trying to keep the diamonds. At the end of the process the diamonds and a few remaining stones were sealed into tin cans. I think the cans were a security thing and this guy came on a helicopter from this company called De Beers to the ship and took the tins away. I thought it was odd that you could buy a tin of diamonds. But you take a risk as it could be pebbles, or full of diamonds because this diamond mining ship, it's automatic, it isn't always going to filter out all the pebbles. But it seems that this is the usual way to buy diamonds, you get a few together that are just as they came from the mines and you then decide what you want to do with them; so you always take a risk when you buy uncut diamonds, they could be worth lots, or not much at all. I expect that the packages that Glazier got were packages of diamonds too. There is this thing called 'blood diamonds' that are diamonds that you shouldn't buy. They are smuggled out of countries and

I wonder if that's what Glazier has as those were not in tins." The Kid looked at both of them in turn for approval at this point and both adults nodded and smiled as the Kid had put the pieces together but the Kid was also coming out of her shell at a time when they could have been allowed to hide. The Consultant tried to wrap this up. He relaxed into his Windsor chair at the head of the kitchen table and mused on what this all could mean.

"So, De Jong's look like a legitimate business but they have a larger value of diamonds than they should have, and they are making loads more money than they should. They are hiding some income somewhere. If they buy a tin from De Beers legitimately and it has loads of diamonds in, then all is good. If it's full of pebbles and worthless, then they 'pretend' that it was actually full of great diamonds as they do get great diamonds through another route; those are the blood diamonds that come in the packets via the back door. Once they are mixed with the legitimately sourced ones they are as good as gold. So they claim to be really good at their job, finding great stones by good fortune, but they are rigging things in their favour." He paused for a moment "but they have got greedy and had more diamonds than they should, perhaps more than they could pass onto the market and held more in their safe, more than five million pounds worth for sure and perhaps they really want them back before anyone realises that they have been importing blood diamonds via Royal Mail." He leaned forward and finished his tea and smiled at them both "that solves a few problems. I couldn't work out who to sell the diamonds to but that's clear now, the De Jongs want them all back desperately enough to pay over the odds and will be happy to do that quickly. I just need to work out a way to do that so that we get our cash, they get their diamonds and we do not get caught." This wasn't a small problem. It's the exchange of cash for goods that opens the possibility for

135

the police to know where the villains will be, too often an appointment is made at a specific spot, at a specific time and dumb criminals are swept up.

He turned his cup on the table and absent mindedly turned things over in his head. The mug had a facsimile of the cover of Swallows and Amazons on it. His favourite book and his favourite cup. If he wanted to engineer an exchange it would be dangerous, the police would be rubbing their hands with glee at the prospect. "If we are to get away with an exchange then I will have to have a think on how we do that."

37

Patience is an overlooked skill within the police force, the senior ranks, press, politicians and general public may all want urgent results and instant justice, but the rank-and-file officers know that often you have to wait for things to progress or unravel for progress to be made. Grace and Harper's favourite way to wait was over an ice-cream when the weather was favourable and with muffins when not. And today the weather was favourable so they had stopped at Central Cross Drive and rifled through the ice creams in the freezer and took a seat on a bench overlooking the expanse of Pittville Park, somewhat denuded of foliage and colour at this time of the year. Harper fondly remembered when such waiting would occur in smoke filled pubs, chatting over cases, football and women; but this was progress and now they sat in the fresh air, with weak sunshine whilst chatting over cases *with* a woman.

Regarding the diamond case, active leads had dried up. Nothing had been seen of the window cleaner and his bank accounts, flat and passport were unused. The Consultant wasn't under active surveillance, which would cost a fortune and should their bosses or his solicitor find out that they had an unsanctioned eye on him disciplinary action would follow. So, they had some 'eyes on' should anyone happen to spot him and the force tried to keep their intelligence up to date with his 'known associates' but the guy was associated with most of the villains of the town.

"Any idea Harps on when those diamonds are going to surface?"

"I did check in with De Beers this week and they still have nothing but it was a different body who I talked to and they talked about 'continuing ongoing vigilance' so they seem to have lobbed our case into the general pile of looking out for bad diamonds. I don't know if we are going to progress this PR or post AR." Grace turned and looked quizzical at the acronyms used and Harper explained "pre or after my retirement."

"You enjoy this too much" said Grace indicating with her little plastic spoon the park but also alluding to their relationship "and you'd miss the excitement." She looked over and Harps had finished his lolly and rolled his eyes. If he had less to worry about he could happily fall asleep soon; but then his phone rang and he pulled a face as he left his reverie. He announced himself in a rather gruff manner and then responded in monosyllabic prompts, such as 'when', 'how long' and 'where' then hung up.

"PR it is then. We have had a ransom note handed in for those diamonds!" His eyes sparkled with the news. "I have an address in The Park where the ransom note was delivered." He *would* miss the excitement.

38

Nigel Jenkins was at the posh end of normal. He drove a Porsche and lived in The Park in Cheltenham. A nice part of a nice part of the world. He was happy with his lot in life and didn't want for much, just tidiness. 'Tidy' extended to the garden where he had a sizeable gravel drive, colourful borders, a small (stripey in fine weather) lawn and good hedges and fencing. He particularly liked the railway sleepers used on-end to demarcate drive and garden. The gravel contrasted and complemented the sleepers, hinting at groins on a beach, but also with the Cotswold stone of the house. They were practical too and ensured that the gravel stayed off the garden but seasonal leaves and petals would happily come the other way, but he wouldn't splash out on a gardener, that was an extravagance too far and finding someone as fastidious as himself tended to be difficult.

He scrunched up the driveway and left the car pinking as it cooled and strode the short way to the porticoed porch and on finding the front door still locked, he opened up and shouted for his wife and received no response. He sat on the stairs and removed his shoes and put them away in a cupboard and then returned to the mail at the front door. There was more direct mail and flyers. He was getting more of this at the moment. Perhaps he should get one of those stroppy signs about 'no circulars' for the letter box. But that would be unsightly. He flicked through the leaflets for conservatories, stair lifts and kebabs and went to the kitchen to put them into the recycling. There was also an intriguing manila A4 envelope that had some bulk to it. He turned it over in his hands and then placed it on the marble counter and as he was near the knife block slit the unaddressed envelope open and tipped out the contents.

Puzzlement was the first impression as a bundle of £50 notes came out. This was the first thing he picked up. He inspected them closely to see if they were real. Ten of them, in a band, with a printed note attached that simply read *'Best not to mention this payment. It is for your inconvenience, services rendered and to evidence that this is a serious approach'*. That piqued his interest as he turned to a sheet of A4 and read the printed text.

To whom it may concern. You have been selected at random to act as a go-between to allow the reparation of diamonds to DJD ltd. Please pass this letter to DJD via the police immediately.

Payment of the equivalent of six million pounds in bitcoin should be made to this wallet address [and details were provided] *before 16:30 on Thursday this week. Delays past that point will result in no further contact. There will be no negotiation. This is a full and final offer. **All** the diamonds will be returned via this randomly selected member of the public on Thursday at 16:30.*

DJD should make a payment of one bitcoin on receipt of this letter to show that this message has been received and understood.

Nigel read the letter twice and there was another sheet of paper with a picture of a copy of The Times with some tin cans. If you looked carefully you could also see a pile of diamonds. Small, cut, shiny ones and Nigel realised that this was 'proof of life' as the paper and headline would show the writer of the letter did have the diamonds and on that date. Wow. He looked through it all again and noted the word 'immediately' and rang the police. He then hid the £500.

39

Harper liked the in and out driveway, he liked the Porsche, he liked the (currently bare) silver birch in the central garden feature that formed a roundabout to drive around but also shielded the frontage from the road and he liked the feel of the garden. It was all very lovely. He rang the bell and was welcomed by a thin, middle-aged, bespectacled man, wearing a suit but his tie was pulled down a bit as an indication that he was home and relaxed; but not too relaxed as the police were coming. He was also in slippers so relaxed was winning out. Harper took the offered hand and stepped into the house and was asked to "remove his shoes please." Harper took a look around as if to check he wasn't entering a mosque or Shinto temple and plainly stated "No, this isn't a social call and we are the police, we are not walking about in our socks." Grace then swept in with a cordial smile and got off to a much better start and that seemed to settle the arrangement of the very nice cop and the grumpy old cop. And that set up suited Harper.

They progressed through the ground floor of the house and were led into another show kitchen overlooking another nice garden and on the table was the ransom demand. Harper took photos then pushed the papers with the aid of tweezers into evidence bags and they both then examined the documents thoroughly. Harper had to be convinced the letter wasn't a hoax and the picture convinced him that this was something of import. He launched into why they were at this particular house.

"So, the letter says you were 'selected at random'. Nothing is random. Why were you selected?" All the while Nigel had hovered in his slippers but he responded to the question promptly by unfolding his arms, shrugging his shoulders, opening his hands and shaking his head to emphasise his response.

"I have no idea. I read about this in the news, that's all." Grace chimed in.

"You don't have any connections to the diamond market?" There was an emphatic head shake and grimace "and have you ever been in trouble with the police?" offered Harper; "no" was the spluttered response.

"Can I ask what you do for a living?" asked Grace heading off in another tangent. It seemed that Nigel was an accountant for an aeronautics manufacturer. Not a big one, just one of the many in the Bristol, Swindon, Cheltenham triangle that manufactured and supplied parts to the medium sized ones who then make big bits for the big ones. He had been employed at the same place many years, was on the board and was doing well; thank you very much. Harper tried another angle.

"Do you know about bitcoin, do you have bitcoin, does your business use bitcoin, do you use foreign currencies at your business?" These were not all asked in a machine gun fashion but each separate question was answered by the same headshake and "no" until the last one where overseas contractors, subsidiaries, purchasers and sales transactions led onto accounts in euros and US dollar denominations. But nothing seemingly untoward. Grace asked if he had a printer in the house. Harper liked that line of questioning and Nigel responded in the affirmative. They asked for a list of the full names and dates of birth of everyone in the household and asked that he print that out a few times so that all the printers in the house were used. They could compare the print and markings to the ransom note.

"Do I need a solicitor?" Harper considered responding to Nigel with his quip about buying a house but kept his grumpy cop persona going and simply asked. "Who is your solicitor?" Grace and Harper awaited an answer but were disappointed that it wasn't the high-profile criminal solicitor that they had recently tangled with. They wanted to establish any connection to anybody else involved in the case.

"I suppose it's the solicitor we used to write our will."

Harper couldn't help but roll his eyes. Grace was more placatory, "then I don't think we need to bother them unless you need to change your will. I think we..." and at that Grace motioned to Harper to include him in the statement "...are coming to the conclusion that you *were* selected at random and the print out will help eliminate you from our enquiries."

Nigel headed off, phone in hand to sort out the print outs. The police decided to get the De Jongs in on this now and potentially kill several birds with one large paving stone. They called papa De Jong and told him to come to them now as they had a development and to get Jane his accountant/daughter-in-law to do the same. Accountancy was the only flimsy link so far.

They sent a photo of the letter into their forensic accountant contact and asked them to look into the account details provided in the instructions. Grace made a quick call to the chief to let her know of the development and stated that they had no obvious links between Nigel, the De Jongs or the thieves, but Thursday that week was the deadline. Nigel dutifully returned with three print outs from his own and his son's printers and they went into an evidence bag with a menacing warning from Harper that concluded with "we will be looking into your background and your wife's and your children. If there is anything that you need to tell us it would be good for you to save us all time and mention it now." He did seem genuinely affronted and stated with a bit of an initial squeak (that took the edge of his affront) that he "was a law-abiding citizen and had nothing to hide." As usual in these situations Grace came to the rescue and she may have even batted her eyelashes as she thanked Nigel "for all his help and was concerned for the bother that he would be under this week with this unfortunate circumstance being forced upon him" and "would he be alright?" He stated that he would, and even gave a deferential bow in Grace's direction for her condescension and then went to make them a coffee. Grace asked for a white instant "if it was no bother" and Harper really wanted a double shot expresso but decided that he had a persona to maintain and asked for the same. The coffees arrived as the doorbell rang.

"Should I get that?"

"Well, it's your house" responded Harper with a heavy hint of 'that's a daft question' in his intonation and then under his breath to Grace as they rose to watch the initial encounter between De Jong and Nigel "and I'm not the butler."

There wasn't any glimmer of recognition, just a genial but awkward welcome (it was a strange situation) and shake of the hand. De Jong strode into the house when he spotted Grace. Nigel nearly plucked up the courage to ask for shoe removal, he really wanted everyone to take their shoes off but had lost the battle on that.

"Mr De Jong. Good to see you and there has been a development, but can I ask before we progress…" he was shown into a seat opposite the police "…have you been to this house or met Mr Jenkins before?" De Jong seemed to take the question seriously and swivelled to look again at Nigel before stating that 'he had not' and then a gentle query 'why am I here?' and they promptly showed him the letter and he took his time to read it.

"And this was addressed to this man?" he indicated to Nigel who was stood at the kitchen island.

"Yes, in an unaddressed envelope. It does seem that Mr Jenkins has been randomly selected to be involved in the exchange."

"Is that unusual. A bit strange?"

Grace and Harper looked at one another for confirmation and agreed that it was. The doorbell rang again and Harper went to watch this welcome. Again, there was no recognition but Nigel was warming to the attention and this strange situation. He was also pleased to see another attractive woman coming into his house. He held Jane's hand a little too long and then invited her to "come and join the party" and showed her into the kitchen. He didn't even consider asking Jane to remove her shoes and looked sulkily at her heels as he escorted her into the kitchen.

"Mrs De Jong" started Harper "can I ask if you have

been here before or have met Mr Jenkins?"

"I don't think we've had the pleasure" said Nigel in a very smarmy way.

"No" was the answer to the first question and then some hesitation "do you have daughters at the Ladies' College?" that was answered in the negative and an explanation that he had "two boys at Pate's" and then Jane asked "are you an accountant?" and on the affirmative answer the penny dropping and Jane stated "I think we have been to the institute meetings so we have been in the same room at times, but I wouldn't say we have met." So that seemed to be all. No connections yet from this guy to the robbery other than a middle-class meeting of professionals over cheap wine and questionable cheddar. Harper offered a chair next to her father-in-law and the letter was then read and the police listened intently to the exchange.

"Six million in less than a week and in bitcoin. It's doable if we get the insurers onboard now." Jane summarised the requirements well and seemed upbeat, perhaps old man De Jong less so.

"Do you think that they will go for it, should we rely on them or try and raise it another way. Loans against the houses for example?"

"The insurers have been dithering but if they help us here they have an upside. They give us five million, which they may plan to do at some point anyway, but this way they have the opportunity to have it back promptly if we get our diamonds back. They may hope never to give us the cash, over some technicality, but then we sue and ensure no-one in the industry uses them again. Insurance is full of gamblers and I would want them to see that this is a way of having an upside. They could help us get the diamonds back. I can set up loans as a contingency for any balance that we cannot pull from our funds" she looked at the police at this point "the family will pull together and pool resources to get the ransom and borrow if we have to. We will have to be quick as moving such a large amount into bitcoin and transferring it isn't run of the mill. We would need the police's help to clear the transactions, there will be lots of banking regulations that we may contravene."

'*Amazing*' thought Grace. Not even a consideration for not paying. They really wanted to get their diamonds back. Perhaps Mr De Jong caught her surprise and so commented "this does afford us the best way to catch those involved doesn't it? You can be at the exchange and stop the money transfer at some point and we can have the diamonds back *and* not lose our money?"

Grace took a moment as she could not be dogmatic on the outcome here so she went for generalisations. "This is the breakthrough we wanted and we have the ransom demand, the choice of involving Mr Jenkins and the statement that Mr Jenkins will be involved in the exchange is new evidence that was not in our hands a few hours ago. There are lots of leads for us to go at. I would never advise to pay any ransom. You risk supporting criminals and throwing good money after the loss you have already experienced. I would suggest you leave this to the police to progress." Mr De Jong seemed to be considering options.

"As we stand now we have lost our diamonds and we could also lose the insurance payout. We don't have that payout either currently. So I would say that we plan to get that and chase this loss with it. Plus a million of our own money. We will then rely on the police to catch the culprits at the exchange or stop the money, or something." He jabbed a finger at the last paragraph of the letter and said "Jane, send the single bitcoin. Let's buy some time."

40

The pressure was on. Grace and Harper may have wished for this eventuality (as they had no other leads or foreseeability of getting a positive solution to the crime) but now that an opportunity had availed itself, they were in the cross hairs if this didn't result in a positive outcome. The chief was most vociferous as it was clear after her own meeting with the De Jongs that they wanted to pay the ransom (something that was usually never countenanced) so she really wanted that strategy to only be seen as bait for an arrest. The chief was clear that if paying the reward was seen as a 'success' then the police had failed. Grace didn't feel that mentioning the propensity for large corporations to pay ransomware attackers or for governments to arrange deals to release their citizens would have defused the chief's mood.

The De Jongs piled in with frequent asks on what progress the police had made with the new clues as they were laying a large bet that this was all going to result in an arrest, they really did have skin in the game and even Harper had some sympathy for their enquiries.

The press knew that something was afoot due to the police presence at the Jenkins house. It was decided that the police should take a close look at the family and get set for all eventualities on Thursday. As more people became involved the story got out and then there were calls for press conferences, statements and access to the investigating officers and that was met with an injunction and gagging order so that the news wasn't leaked and an even bigger posse of onlookers attracted to the circus. All a distraction, but the chief *would* have enjoyed the limelight, but for the prospect of it all going tits up.

And there was added pressure as the new leads from the letter and demand had not gone far. Nigel Jenkins and family did seem to be quite normal. Normal porn on their computers, normal clean police records, normal employment, normal bank accounts and, like normal people, they were not listed as known associates for criminals. Their printers had not created the ransom letter. They had gone for a deep dive into the background to ensure that Nigel and family were not involved in the robbery in some way and the checks came up clean. They did seem to have been selected at random. Harper had said 'nothing is random' but he didn't mean it. The police were well aware of the 'random attacks' where completely innocent individuals were involved in violent crime. It happens. Bad things happen to good people. It did make detection difficult and the whole force was happy that, statistically, your assailant would know you. In this instance it also complicated things. In a 'usual' ransom situation the training was clear, open lines of communication and stall. Give small concessions to build bridges and trust and stall some more. Wear them down and await them giving up. Here there was no-one to communicate and negotiate with. They seemed to be in a take-it-or-leave-it situation and the De Jongs were keen to take it.

There was a big concern (due to the keenness of the De Jongs to pay) that this was a ruse and an elaboration of the inside job. Make it look like your diamonds were stolen, but have the family take them, fake the insurance claim and then get the diamonds back via the ransom...which they would also keep. Two things made this unlikely; nothing untoward had led the police to this being an inside job (and they had looked really hard at that from day-one) and the insurers were adamant that they owned the diamonds once they paid the claim. If the diamonds were ever recovered then they wanted their cash back.

The forensic accountant and National Crime Agency swung into action on the bitcoin wallet details provided within the letter. The wallet seemed to belong to a shipping business registered in the Philippines. They tried to find out more but the business was ultimately fictitious. The wallet was very real, had existed for six months and now held one bitcoin. Just finding out this detail took an extended time due to time-zone and language differences plus the legalities of data protection…time ticked by as they ultimately got no-where with that lead.

The letter itself and envelope were stock items that you could buy from branches of WH Smith. Such a high-street brand had lots of CCTV but also had lots of branches. There was no forensics on the paper, the days of licking stamps and envelopes was over and mourned by the police as that good source of DNA had evaporated. The printer was an inkjet printer using a very ordinary Epson cartridge. This did give the prospect of trying to match a print cartridge to the letter text and that could have been promising until it was pointed out the ease with which print cartridges are replaced. Again the demise of, good-old-fashioned type writers was mourned. The De Jongs did have a good look at the photo within the letter, the one that showed The Times, some tins and something that looked like diamonds. The newspaper itself wasn't very clear in the photo but clear enough to see what day it was produced. They were happy that the few diamonds shown and the tins were like those they lost. They were clear that these were the type of cut stones that they had taken from raw, then selected, cut and polished. There were no un-cut diamonds in the photo and that was the bulk of what was taken. They explained that they bought the tins from the Namibian offshoot of De Beers and explained the potluck nature of opening them to see what had been dredged and sorted before being sealed in a tin for security in transportation. They explained that it was far easier to take a few stones from a pile of stones without raising any suspicion, but a missing numbered tin was soon spotted in the multiple audits and reconciliations that De Beers made from when the cans were sealed to their purchase.

So, it all seemed to be coming down to Thursday. No expense had been spared planning a hidden cordon around the Jenkin's house. Their phone line had been tapped and all visitors were turned away by uniformed police at the end of the driveway. The family were being put up in a hotel while the police searched the house and only Nigel would come back on Thursday to play whatever part he needed to play.

Perhaps their last line of defence was their pulling in resources from GCHQ to assist. They had a plan to follow the money from the crypto wallet to its ultimate destination. They should be able to see clues to where the perpetrators were operating from. That seemed odd to Harper as he had always thought that the perpetrators were close at hand, somewhere in leafy Cheltenham. Now that crypto currencies were in the mix bad actors throughout the world seemed to have a look-in of being involved.

As the new leads petered out Grace and Harper found time to have a coffee and muffin and take in the air. They went to The Suffolks as it was nearby and walked the perimeter of the grand square. It was definitely off-season for the bowls club within the square. Mist and cold preceded a darkening lunchtime. They took a seat in the steamed window of a coffee shop overlooking St James church where pizza was the only thing being celebrated now.

"I was hopeful when we had a message of an exchange but I can't say I am hopeful now." Harper considered an optimistic reply and struggled.

"We live in hope that someone will turn up with a bag full of diamonds and we have a live suspect; plus we follow the money and get the cash back and get more suspects from that trail."

"Or no diamonds turn up and the cash disappears. I did

ask the pointy headed GCHQ team how often they catch ransomware criminals. It seems that they don't get the big fish. When money enters a government-run bank it evaporates; that's the norm for big ransomware attacks. They do catch the little fish, kids in their parent's back bedrooms mainly."

"That's handy ma'am as we were already looking for a little person to fit into that Trojan toolbox. Perhaps this whole thing is a spotty teen, in their bedroom, on a PC?"

"Are you back on your theory that we should lock up all teenagers for the duration of their teens?"

"And slash crime rates in a moment. I will do it when I'm elected president of the UK." There was a pause after the gallows humour.

"Do you think this will work out Harps?"

"No idea ma'am. No idea."

41

Thursday came around with a surety that was missing from many other aspects of the case. The scene was set and players assembled. Grace took a tour of the Jenkins' kitchen firstly visiting Nigel and his wife (who wouldn't be excluded from the excitement and was along for moral support and in-charge of catering). Mr Jenkins was hating the mess and wondered if his flooring would ever be the same again. This pair had placed themselves in the kitchen part of the kitchen-diner and were responsible for dispensing tea, coffee, cake and snacks. This was a good diversion for them as there was no knowing what part this 'randomly selected' party had to play. For all the investigating that the police had done into the family nothing had been found linking them to any other part of the inquiry.

Sat at the island counter with laptops, black boxes and

copious wires stretching to power sockets were the GCHQ bods. They had travelled in a pair, young, bright and eager to help. Their skillset was to trace the money and any calls. They had explained their plan. The had a program that would trace the path of the payment automatically and gather information as it went completing a comprehensive audit trail. They could sit back and watch and also automatically seize the funds when the money came into the UK banking bailiwick. Grace had a soft spot for the taller one who seemed eminently geeky, polite and she was sure he had some James Bond hidden within him. Very well hidden thought Harper. Once they were set up and monitoring they chatted freely with all in the room.

That was unlike the NCA duo who stayed by the seats overlooking the garden near the conservatory. They talked to one-another in hushed tones, made a few furtive looks about but they kept themselves to themselves. The female of the pair had participated fully in the briefing and knew that their role was liaison should this escalate past the resources and reach of Gloucestershire police. As the diamond market was worldwide their broader vista may be needed. And they had government links should that be needed. Their aloofness was fine as they each looked like they had been trained to kill with a spoon.

The De Jongs had come in numbers and had felt at home at the dining table. Papa at the head with his sons to right and left. Jane had attended too and had a laptop open and ready. Apart from the police they seemed the most nervous as they had much to lose.

The police contingent was large, but most of their bodies were in concentric rings about the property and Cheltenham trying to be alert to many possibilities. Within the kitchen was the chief, her PA and a PC who would act as the link to the control room. That group were perched on sofas in the TV part of the kitchen-diner using it as a monitor shared with the control room. As time had ticked on less notice was paid to it and the chief and her PA were currently planning speeches to cover most eventualities.

So, Grace nodded and checked in with the groups as she did her rounds and then handed Harper a Hob Nob and sat beside him on the hall stairs and checked her watch.

"The De Jongs planned the transfer for fourteen hundred. I wonder if that will be the last they see of their money. They still seem very set on doing this." Harper jotted a note and responded.

"I think they want all their diamonds back. The word 'all' was underlined in the ransom note and they were quick to agree to this payment. You know that I have a list of oddities in this case. Do you know that we have not seen what was stolen. We saw an empty safe and a photo of some tins and sparkly diamonds, but we are told what was stolen were uncut diamonds. I don't even know what they would look like. Usually when something is nicked a car, antiques, cash, we know what it looks like, but this is a pile of something we have never seen. Another concern is the wealth of the De Jongs so perhaps that's the link. They want *all* their diamonds. They said it was five million pounds worth, but they, quick as a flash, were happy to pay six so they must be worth more than that *and* by enough distance to take this chance."

"But we have nothing on the De Jongs and if this whole thing was make-believe then why give away their insurance payout?"

"That's also on the 'I don't know' pile along with why we are here with this randomly selected guy. I get that it has put distance between the thieves and us but why this guy. We were told twice that this is random. Why even mention that but to plant the seed that this had no connection to the crime? Everyone we have looked at for this has either no connection or disappeared. So their window cleaner and my old safe cracking mate are in that group. But we have nothing. And we are pinning high hopes on the GCHQ bods to trace that cash and collect evidence along the way. This could slip through our fingers."

Grace tried to lighten the mood and gave Harper a friendly punch on the shoulder "c'mon Harps, we have been waiting for a mistake and the more actors in play then the more likely it is that there will be a mistake of some nature and then we reel them in. All we need is a plausible link to the Consultant and we can drag him in and search his place; that would lighten your mood." Harper nodded, that was another someone who had eluded his grip for too long "let's get ready for the payment."

The De Jongs were stood in a huddle, evidently agreeing that they were 'go'. As they nodded agreement and started to take their seats the chief felt it her place to re-iterate that paying a ransom was against her and the force's recommendations and made sure that was recorded by all for posterity so that her arse was adequately covered in any fall-out and inquiry. And then it came down to a few clicks. Jane took control and swiftly typed passwords and with a few mouse moves looked at old man De Jong who closed his eyes and gave an emphatic nod. There were a few more clicks and then the laptop was closed and everyone swivelled slowly to look at the cyber experts who were already intently looking at their screens. The crowd physically moved with the focus of their attention in their direction and formed a semi-circle behind them so they also looked at the screens. They didn't like the crowd looking over their shoulders but worked with it and started to give their commentary.

"We followed the packet of data and everything is normal, decrypted on arrival and processed and there it is within the wallet now." There was a pointing at numbers on the screen to evidence this statement. Harper made the mistake of reaching out towards the screen.

"Do you mean that number?"

"Don't touch the screen! Yes. That number. Sheesh." A black look was thrown over their shoulder and a cloth was produced and the smallest of smears removed "and now we wait." It didn't take long. The number started to fall. It was evident that bitcoin was being transferred. "The program is following the transfer now, we can see it's moving to another account." To the uninitiated looking at the screen it seemed like the funds were moving in chunks. Grace asked "what's happening?"

The pointy head thought for a second and sounded a little concerned. "They are moving the money, but it's only in small amounts. We expected one transfer and have a clear trace on the first amount and we will record the rest. His fingers nimbly hit the keys and several more windows of data appeared that were then tessellated. It was clear lots of things were happening simultaneously.

"Don't worry. The trace is completed as we have a destination account for the first amount. It was transferred via a clearing house to this account number. Oh!" There clearly was some surprise.

"What is it?" asked Grace and the question was answered from behind her by Jane who pointed (without touching it) to the screen.

"The money is back where it started, that's the account number we paid the money into." The GCHQ guy seemed non-plussed.

"So, we traced the payment and its gone in a loop. A real red-herring." He seemed flustered "but that's OK we are recording the other movements..." there was a flurry of more keys and fingers with the second guy also keying commands into his computer too. There seemed to be a quick conference and gesticulation that resulted in a definitive comment.

"We hoped that we could track this live and actually see where the money was transferred to. But it has been split into smaller packets and is being transferred numerous times as we watch and all in different directions. We have followed the second package as far as a currency exchange and it seems to have gone into roubles and then to a Russian crypto exchange. So they are moving it through currencies and asset types."

"Russia? So they are involved?" asked Jane with incredulity in her voice and the NCA team's ears pricked up.

"They maybe but by transferring it through Russia our ability to track it or ask for information is diminished" that was from the previously mute GCHQ guy "they are going to some time and expense to cover their tracks as each exchange is losing them money."

"But they had lots to start with" added his colleague and they both shrugged in agreement that hiding the ultimate destination of the cash and ending up with something was going to be a good outcome "so we will be able to trace the transfers by looking at the audit log, but that's going to take some time and it may not actually lead to a final destination." That was said matter-of-factly but Grace asked for clarity.

"You mean you cannot trace it?" the GCHQ guy swivelled in his seat to face the audience. He seemed very relaxed for a man who had lost six million pounds. He turned to his colleague.

"Lex situs?" The response was a shrug and the comment "Omniterritorial." Harper was about to look for a spoon to commit murder with but an explanation was on the way from the two spooks.

"Lex situs refers to the situation when property rights are based on where the object is. So if you have a house or business in England it would be English law but those are tangible and fixed. But here we have crypto tokens, digital objects and they have a unique state of being nowhere and everywhere, at the same time. That's referred to as omniterritorial. Here it looks to have gone into and out of Russia as different currencies, crypto or otherwise, so we are limited on what we can do from a legal jurisdiction viewpoint. And it seems to have been split into multiple packets each of which could be omniterritorial. The good news is that all these transactions give us plenty to look at and follow. We can look for any fingerprints along the way that indicate who may be involved, if they use accounts that have been used in ransomware before for example." He seemed to have come to a halt.

"And how long will that take?" offered Grace.

"Ah, well this looks to be sophisticated and automated, the speed with which the cash has moved is rather impressive and it is going to take some time. But we will get a team right onto it" and with that he closed his laptop lid which didn't go down well. That seemed to be saying 'goodbye' to the cybersecurity team being able to help on this today. There was pandemonium as the chief and De Jongs shouted questions that boiled down to 'where's the money'. Grace was dumbstruck and was extricated by Harper gently pulling on her elbow and escorting her from the mele.

"Let them play their computer games. I didn't have faith that they would do much. How often have ransomware gangs been caught. We need to focus on the exchange. That has always been our best option to see who we are dealing with. If they are going to give up *all* the diamonds something is going to happen soon. Let's see." They levitated towards the randomly selected member of the public and his wife who nervously stood beside their brownies. Grace wanted to see what would transpire and was trying to be optimistic.

"Something will happen. It seems that selling diamonds is a closed shop and difficult. The thieves may just want to get rid of the stolen goods they are holding, in case they are caught red handed."

"Throwing them in the Severn would achieve that though" added the less optimistic Harper.

"But perhaps there is honour amongst thieves. Perhaps they are coming here with the diamonds as we speak." They contacted control and gave them an update and ensured all units were on alert.

It began to get dark, that surprisingly quick autumn darkness that seems too early in the day and the chief was beginning to mutter that 'nothing was going to happen' and 'this was the worst of outcomes' and began looking at her press release again. As the unseen sun passed from behind a grey cloud to being behind the horizon a light drizzle started and joined the early autumn nightfall. The mood dampened as well. It seemed that four-thirty was a defining time and the phone duly rang. It was the landline and they knew that Nigel was not ex-directory so it could be anyone but the timing was significant at exactly half past four.

The communication part of GCHQ was now on point and they swiftly used caller ID and said "it's a call box, I have the number. It's 01242" so that was in the Gloucestershire area code and with a few clicks on their computer... "and I have the location, it's a call box in Guiting Power."

The chief gave a thumbs up to Grace and peeled away to get the closest units to head that way to seal off the phone box and gather evidence.

A nod was given to Nigel who picked up the phone, put it on speaker so that all could hear and then he gave an overly jaunty "hello."

"Are you at number ten The Park?"

"Yes, I am."

"The diamonds are on the driveway. I will repeat that. The diamonds are on the driveway. Please repeat that back to me."

Without understanding Nigel repeated "the diamonds are on the driveway" and with that the line went dead.

That took the wind out of sails as the expectation was that there would be instructions, a conversation, a meet and an exchange. What did that mean?

Harper strode to the front door and went onto the porch and surveyed the scene as others came behind him and Grace took his shoulder.

"Seen anything?" he bellowed at the slightly damp PC stood at the end of the driveway in high vis guarding the blue tape that demarcated that no-one was allowed up the driveway unless permitted.

"Nothing!" was the call back.

"How about you?" called Harper again but this time pointing to the officer on the other side of the road from his colleague. Not only the driveway but the road was closed off so that officer was facing the property from the opposite kerb.

"Nothing here!" was the response.

"The diamonds are on the driveway" repeated Grace to herself quietly. They looked from the shelter of the wide porch at the driveway. Nothing was changed. The Porsche was unmoved, the birch was letting its paper bark peel away, its leaves long gone until spring. The garden still looked good as it approached its winter slumber. Drizzle was becoming rain. It dripped from the foliage making the leaves in the shrubbery shudder and small rivulets formed and rolled down the car and dripped to the ground. It was peaceful but the autumn chill of night would therefore follow. The streetlights began to come on and slowly grew in their intensity. Nigel turned on the exterior lights and pools of light illuminated the driveway, garden and highlighted the structure of the trees. He was proud of his garden.

"The diamonds are on the driveway" softly repeated Grace again and she reached for her torch and a cone of light sprang out from the low steps on which they stood to the Porsche and was then played further down the driveway. The intensity of the light caught the water droplets and reflected the light. The hi-vis of the officers bounced the light back as they looked perplexed and from the gravel in the driveway pinpricks of colourful spectrums of light were reflected.

"The diamonds are on the driveway" said Harper echoing the low tone that Grace had used and chuckled. Papa De Jong burst to the front of the group forcibly dragging his eldest with him as he shouted "the diamonds are on the driveway!" He fell onto the gravel and started to pluck at the stones inspecting those he picked up and stuffing some into his pocket.

Harper called control and explained as best that he could that the exchange had occurred but a tight cordon was needed on the premises as the De Jong family were currently on their hands and knees picking up diamonds from the driveway and they could be at it all night.

Part IV Closedown

42

It was spring half term for posh schools and the Consultant had come to visit the gang. The Kid was being well cared for by Safe's wife and Glazier. She had settled into school well, which is what he had paid highly for. The girls there were nice and the art education excellent and Glazier was trying to become something of a big brother or mentor. He would often say 'you don't want to end up as a window cleaner!' and was keen to ensure the mistakes of his youth, some of which emanated from being in-care were not repeated. The Consultant had his own reasons for keeping the Kid happy and within the tent. She knew what he had done. If Glazier talked he would be in all sorts of trouble with the law himself, but if the Kid talked then she would walk away as the victim that she was; drawn into this by her parent and himself. The more the Kid was part of the family and part of his family business the better. He had not discouraged her working with Safe and Lock in their (now shared) workshop. She had picked up how to pick locks with ease. Perhaps this would be the succession planning that he had been looking out for. Could he retire to this area too and let her carry on the business?

Safe was definitely retired from operational work and was a feature of the locality. He was, literally, a different person here. He spoke like a native and now that he had bronzed like a Mediterranean he looked the part too. His wife missed the shopping of Cheltenham but that was it.

Lock had life ahead of him and while he now had plenty of money he relished the challenges set by Safe and had become the apprentice that the Consultant hoped. Now he would be the go-to for safe cracking and his older friend could retire in peace.

Glazier had been travelling. He had a new passport and name and passed through the airports of the world seeking out new experiences and didn't seem to miss England. When he did miss England he went to Gibraltar or New Zealand and had fish and chips or went to Eire for a night in the pub. He could risk coming back to Cheltenham in the future but seemed happy to travel further afield at the moment.

And so the Consultant sat on a Portuguese villa's veranda and looked across the pool where Safe and Lock sat with a beer each and down over the sand to the littoral edge where Glazier, the Kid and Mrs Safe were just passing time chatting and laughing.

The Consultant was pleased to have made this happen. The money had filtered through enough countries, accounts, denominations and exchanges to hide its source and destination. It ended up being consolidated into Swiss bank accounts for each of them and was clean and ready to use. There was a deduction for himself for the services rendered, plus all the costs of the job itself; but no-one came out of this poor and no-one had been caught.

Being caught always played on his mind on days like today where you could look as far as the horizon. Could he manage years in the nick? Everyone knew that an exchange of stolen goods for cash is fraught with difficulty and he reasoned that very few people knew what uncut diamonds look like. He remembered the safe being opened and not knowing what they had found. It looked like gravel so he set a plan to find similar gravel and he cycled around Cheltenham in an aimless fashion until he found what he needed. It was a large, gravelled area on private land that was the same colour as he needed. He did a trial run. His cover was to deliver junk mail and he walked the length of the road in heavy disguise, posting flyers and then he walked onto the target driveway and surreptitiously allowed a trail of diamonds to fall from his pockets and down his trouser legs. Once on the ground it was well camouflaged and hidden in plain sight. With that check he moved quickly as this was the risk. With the diamonds on the ground and outside of his control all could be lost. Perhaps someone would spot them, or report him loitering and the game would be up; so time was of the essence. He had to make a few trips. He continued to deliver the free paper and junk mail and emptied the diamonds from his pockets and through a hole in the bag he carried his paper in, onto the driveway as he walked in, and out, of the property. On the last day he also delivered the ransom note and the die was cast.

If the De Jongs did not pay then the gang had nothing, no diamonds and no money; but they had also not been caught and that may be the best they could hope for. He had held onto some of the cut diamonds. A few could go onto the market without too much disturbance but potentially, all it would do was cover his costs.

But it did work. The money moved as designed. He wasn't worried that cyber security experts would monitor the transfers as he had employed his own GCHQ cyber security expert to design the system. The call was from a phone box out in the sticks, the Kid had been asked to make the call at four-thirty. Had the money been paid or not, the call would have been placed.

The De Jongs stopped smuggling diamonds and worked on filtering in their amassed amount of gems into the market. That was another party happy not to have been caught. They spent a week sieving through the driveway contents and the police did find a bag of cut diamonds hidden in the garden, so most of *all* the diamonds were returned. The insurers had their claim payment back from the De Jongs and were happy at the resolution. They didn't offer a renewal premium.

Perhaps only Grace and Harper didn't fare well from the outcome. It was a robbery and ransom and the perpetrators had got away scot-free. Another dint on Grace's promotion path. Harper had to convince her, once again, that 'you cannot win them all'. When the dust had settled and all hope of progress seemed to be gone (despite another force coming into review the case) he had bought her an ice-cream in the hope that he could cheer her up. He did selfishly think that he was lucky in this. Grace wanted to solve everything, but if she did do that then she would be promoted away from him. He wanted to end his career with Grace. She was the best he had worked with. He would miss her when he retired. He looked over to her gently devouring her Mr Whippy. He looked in a paternal way, which was strange as she did outrank him, but couldn't help smiling softly. Grace looked back.

"Harper are you all-right? If you keep smiling at me like that I'm get a restraining order."

ABOUT THE AUTHOR

The author works and lives in Cheltenham after moving from his childhood home of Gloucester. He works in financial services and IT and has enjoyed writing and storytelling for many years and found the encouragement to publish *Comfy Monkey* (the first Grace and Harper novel) from Liggy Webb and the Montpellier Writers' Group. He is married with three children and has recently gained Zippy the dog.

Printed in Great Britain
by Amazon

56516045R00096